To Save A Child

By

Beatrice Fairbanks Cayzer

To Save A Child

B.F. Cayzer

Copyright © 2015 by B.F. Cayzer.

Paperback: 978-1-953048-15-8

All rights reserved. No part of this book may be used or reproduced by any means, graphic, electronic, or mechanical, including photocopying, recording, taping or by any information storage retrieval system without the written permission of the publisher except in the case of brief quotations embodied in critical articles and reviews.

Because of the dynamic nature of the Internet, any web addresses or links contained in this book may have changed since publication and may no longer be valid. The views expressed in this work are solely those of the author and do not necessarily reflect the views of the publisher, and the publisher hereby disclaims any responsibility for them.

Any people depicted in stock imagery provided by Thinkstock are models, and such images are being used for illustrative purposes only.

Writers Branding
1800-608-6550
www.writersbranding.com
orders@writersbranding.com

Contents

Chapter 1 1

Chapter 2 4

Chapter 3 16

Chapter 4 22

Chapter 5 29

Chapter 6 32

Chapter 7 38

Chapter 8 54

Chapter 9 57

Chapter 10 64

Chapter 11 67

Chapter 12 72

Chapter 13 78

Chapter 14 83

Chapter 15 85

Chapter 16 87

Chapter 17 92

Chapter 18 94

Chapter 19 101

Chapter 20 105

Chapter 21 108

"To Karen Butler who worked on the physical and Economic Development of cities such as New York's Times Square and the former Naval Air Base in Glenview, IL to create better lives and thousands of jobs for their citizens" . . . and who appreciates the need to better the lives of others.

*Also by Beatrice Fairbanks Cayzer**

TALES OF PALM BEACH (as Beatrice de Holguin)
THE PRINCES AND PRINCESSES OF WALES
ROYAL ECCENTRICS (with Barbara Cartland)
ROYAL LOVERS (with Barbara Cartland)
THE ROYAL WORLD OF ANIMALS
DIANE (PRINCESSE DE POLIGNAC)
MURDER BY MEDICINE
THE HAPPY HARROW MURDER TRILOGY
MURDER TO MUSIC
MURDERED MOTHERS
MURDER IN MARRIAGE
VAMPIRE MURDERS
LOVE LOVE IN DARFUR
THE HARROW QUARTET
MURDER FOR MUNITIONS
MODELS MURDERED IN MILAN
MOCKING MURDERS IN MADRID
MEXICO'S MOVIELAND MURDERS
MURDER FOR BEAUTY
THE SECRET DIARY OF MRS. JOHN QUINCY ADAMS

Like a prisoner on Death Row, I asked myself some telling questions. I was standing in Louisville's daunting April wind, my old Eton two-shades-of-blue scarf wound around my out-thrust neck. I stretched to watch our string's best racehorse do his morning gallops at Kentucky's Churchill Downs. Not even the thrill of seeing him outpace the competition could blot the shame at permitting my darling wife to be threatened by a serial killer.

Why had I acted so stupidly? Why couldn't I have protected better the girl I loved? Why in Heaven's name didn't I twig to *who* was the murderer?

Looking back, the outcome seems so obvious. Yet I'd failed to twig. My name is Rick Harrow, I'm British-born, a racehorse trainer by profession. In this winter of discontent it seemed that almost everything that could go wrong went wrong. Three of my long time Owners died within months of one another. None of the heirs wanted to keep racehorses in training: the horses were sold too quickly, and at a loss.

Happy, aka Hillary, my Kentucky Hills-born wife, shook her head in disbelief: "Ah cain't comprehend all them fancy folks what don't wanna train with yo-all. We'uns down to a One-Owner stable!" What Happy referred to was actually a couple, Lord and Lady Cabrach, who raced in the name of Frances Cabrach, because it was Fran who paid for our vet, the upkeep, and the entry fees of their horses.

Desperate to pay the bills at our Epsom cottage, pay the head stable lad, and pay a fulltime live-in nanny for our three kids, I'd agreed to be headhunted to work as Assistant Trainer for a Kentucky Derby-winning racehorse Trainer called Mike McAdoo. I liked him fine, and would have worked for him forever if I hadn't got involved with Happy's input to catch a serial killer. Happy, an apprentice jockey, moonlighted as a sleuth and had netted serial killers before.

"This heah one be the bottom of the pit," she declared, tossing her blond curls the morning we flew to California for the late summer racing there.

I couldn't agree more. Except, that case led to another one that actually implicated President Putin of Russia. How come? Leave it to my Kentucky Hills-born wife to upset *President Putin's strategy!*

President Putin! That master strategist, and magician.

Chapter 1

Making love in London spells rapture. Happy and I always had our best sex in unfamiliar beds.

Maybe it was due to fish and chips in my tummy, real whisky – not that bastard bourbon – plus a now-very-willing wife who constantly trembled from the cold English climate which I could modify by taking her into my arms.

No blue pill needed to battle the dreaded ED.

We'd returned to our Epsom cottage after doing our thing in California. We'd barely had a chance to joyfully rejoin our children and happily rev up my stable with the sudden appearance of a surge of new Owners, when we'd both been summoned to meet Lord Cabrach in London.

He'd booked us into London's Goring Hotel, where we'd been warned to expect to pack our bags for another trip across the pond.

We liked the huge central garden of this hotel, although tiny snow flakes -- like sugar – now powdered the leaves of its mature trees.

The hotel had long been famous for its collection of toy lambs. Its public relations apex occurred when Kate Middleton left from its quiet doors to ride to Westminster Abbey for her wedding to Prince William. Prior to that national hurrah, most of its fame rested on the fact its doors were a mere few hundred yards from a back entrance to Buckingham Palace's garden.

Why, London? We'd have preferred to book into a B&B near the Earl's seat, near Oxford, to more easily do our morning and evening gallops with our string of racehorses.

We soon had that WHY answered, meeting with a Peer of Britain in the hotel's cozy bar.

It was warmed by a welcoming fire, scented from apple boughs falling into embers. The Peer cuddled in a huge armchair, like a baby kangaroo in its mother's pouch. He was reading The DAILY MAIL from a rack of free newspapers for customers, the yard-long wood pole keeping its pages in order.

This Peer of the Realm happened to be one of my racehorse Owners. Correctly titled the Earl of Cabrach, he'd retained connections with MI5 from his hush-hush past. Why had he summoned us to London, and arranged our stay at this hotel?

We'd been instrumental in repairing his love life up to the point where he'd married the world famous contralto, Fran Purcell, and had rewarded us ever since with a friendship extending far beyond a Trainer and jockey relationship.

He gave me a bear hug, and lowered his head toward his neck for Happy as if in the presence of HM The Queen. "What! No California tans?" he barked.

"We were busy, Jeremy." I said, accepting a ready glass of whisky.

"Found us'n a preteen girl locked alive in a coffin," Happy put in, helping herself to a handful of mixed nuts from the bar's shiny oak top.

"Exactly. That story made PRIVATE EYE." Jeremy's right hand swooped into the bowl of nuts, following Happy's lead. He lowered his voice that had been as welcoming as a foghorn searching for a lost barge. "My bosses have need for that sort of help. How about going to a conference in Oxfordshire where the guest of honor will fill you in what the plan is."

"Plan fo' what?" Happy interrupted. "We'uns got kids 'n hosses wut needs us by Epsom!"

Happy's eyebrows swooped like a seagull's wings avoiding a hawk.

I echoed, like a parrot learning new words, "Kids and horses."

"Happy, I have the greatest respect for your duties as a mother. And, yours as a Dad, Rick. But I'm deeply touched by an immense humanitarian problem torturing the U.S.A, and have involved myself in one way to minimize it. Starting tomorrow, with this conference."

"Us'n ain't goin' home to Epsom?" Happy moaned.

I said nothing, in the British way of asking for more details.

Jeremy gave us details. "I cannot tell you much about this until you have signed up to help. I've taken the liberty of ordering a limo for you and the kids to go to a seat in Oxfordshire belonging to my old friend Freddy. Nice sort of chap, not at all grand although his Ducal title comes straight down from Charles the Second. A Russian fellow, Hannibal Kash, Freddy met on a shoot, has offered to underwrite both the conference and an overnight dinner party. Well, I'd better not say more. Freddy has leased his seat for the conference, and the dinner, although he has a party of PGs to shoot pheasants the next day. Freddy's estate was chosen because he has the best dog handler south of Edinburgh."

"Dawg handluh? Ah's t' work with a dawg handlah?"

"No. Not exactly," Jeremy tried a sad little laugh, like a child on his first day of school. "Trust me. You are wanted because you are adept at catching killers. The dog handler has a sideline in using his fire-and-rescue dog to save victims buried by earthquakes or under burned out buildings." With that he returned The DAILY MAIL to its rack, and left us.

We didn't get a fancy dinner. After Jeremy left us we ordered crab sandwiches: 'Cheap and cheerful,' I had a beer, not sure whether the unknown man underwriting tomorrow's conference would be paying for our food bill in addition to paying for our night at the Goring Hotel. We were going to skip a pudding, when the owner of the hotel – *the Mr. Goring* -- came to our small table *a deux* to greet us and told the waiter to bring sponge cake for us "on the house."

"I'm the third generation to own this hotel," he remarked, filling us in on its history, "I hope you like our sponge cake. And take a look at the statues in the lobby. Made by my daughter."

The owner rocked away like a tugboat. He abandoned us in favor of a movie star who had just entered the bar.

Happy's eyes lit up. "Cain't remembuh huh name, but Ah seen huh on Turner Movie Classics. Wow! Who'd have thought Ah'd be in the same room as the likes o' a real lahve cel'brity."

I hurried Happy to the lift, worried that she might go up and beg for an autograph. I recalled very well how she had flipped over movie stars on our first trip to California, like a hick just off the bus in glitterland.

Then came the rapture in our bedroom. Bliss.

Chapter 2

Next morning promptly at ten the limo arrived that Jeremy had spoken of.

Fresh from California's unremitting sunshine, we'd brought very few clothes suitable for England's climate. What we did have was more suitable for a day at Santa Anita's races than for a stay-over at a first-class hotel. Both of us being very prompt by nature, we rushed down to the lobby, glanced at the vaunted statues, bolted into the limo, and put our feet up on our tired flight-weary suitcases to settle down.

Our three children were asleep on the limo's matching sofas that stretched horizontally the length of its passenger section. Like mother and father grouse, we were ulta careful not to disturb our 'chillun." Much as we loved them, we needed an hour of respite from stress before what promised to be a challenging evening.

London gave us a gray day. Rain pelted the limo's windows like the fugue of a toccatta. Asleep, Happy was oblivious of the spotty rain. Her soft breath hung like a pink sunset's cloud to glide gently over our three children.

Suddenly, half way to Oxford, Happy was awakened by our children scampering for her lap. The two littlest grabbed for her calves like baby trurtles heading for the ocean.

Tim went straight for her lap.

I never have been a hands-on father. I preferred to play the icon. When appeals came to referee arguments or to lay down the law, then I would invoke the necessary. I never finessed Happy. She was the Supreme Court in our family.

Joy had been unleashed when we entered the limo to find our three kids there, although asleep. We had seen them for only two days before being summoned to London. Between glimpsing with radiant looks at each other, we'd sat for a good hour with our feet on the suitcases until Happy had that short kip.

It was Timmy who woke her up with his shouts of glee at seeing us on board and then roused his brother and sister.

The rain outside the limo would have been ignored even if shafts of gold, for all we cared. When all's said and done, the members of this Harrow family love one another's company. That is to say, when we are already awake.

As we approached the Duke's grounds, the gloomy rain stopped, leaving a bitter, unpromising gray sky.

Built of granite, Freddy's home was no Ducal Palace, but rather a middle-sized manor house that had perhaps served the estate's Factor in the pre-wars flush days. Its tall entrance could have permitted the entry of a carriage. There was a messy hand-lettered sign.

It had two arrows, one pointing left for KENNELS, the other pointing right for MAIN HOUSE.

Another fifty yards and our limo stopped in the deep tracks left by heavier vehicles, the majority of which were Range Rovers ready for the shooting party's guns and dogs. Our limo didn't stop at the front door because its Sixteenth Century carved doors had buckled, and were muzzled by two large planks. Cobwebs on the dead panels gave notice that this was not the way to fires and tea.

Another messy sign read: "No guns permitted in the main house. All guns and ammo to be handed in to Security Office for location in safe." 'Safe' had been spelled with two ffs.

There was no welcoming butler. No staff visible. This Duke's amenities were for pheasant shooting, with no extras.

Our limo driver lowered our suitcases to the gravel driveway, opened the boot of the car and removed our kids' paraphernalia:a tricycle, three teddybears, a ball for soccer, and bags full of the kids' necessities such as tooth brushes, combs, pajamas, and changes of clothes.

Happy pushed the sleepy kids toward a half-timbered door from which an amber light wavered through artistic colored glass fit for a church. "C'mon, yo-all, no fidgitin' yo-all be res-pon-sible fo' each o' yourn things." Happy flapped her arms like a mother partridge ushering her young away from a predatory falcon.

I tipped our surly driver. He drove away in a fountain of pebbles. I fitted our suitcases under my armpits – two for Happy, one for me – and lumbered toward the colored glass sending a kaleidoscope of tints to become glittering sequins on the hardened snow. I closed the door to preserve the slight warmth from an open hearth enriched with no more than one weary lump of coal.

"Anyone here?"

At my call a tall, young man appeared, wearing nothing but the formal striped trousers suitable for a butler serving dinner. His hairy chest embarrassed him. He tried to cover his nipples, one with each hand.

"Sorry, Sir," he breathed. "We were told nobody would arriive until after lunch."

"Do thet mean there ain't no lunch? Nothin' fo' the kids?" Happy shook herself like a hungry parrot ruffles its feathers. "We ain't got no car fo' to go into Oxfo'd fo' vittels."

Patting Happy's hand, I suggested: "Maybe we can order in some pizza."

The half-naked butler gave clucking noises like when a lovebird entices a mate. He covered one bare foot with the other, and said: "Know just the place, Sir. Got the number from the boys who brought in our company's food. There had been no food provided for us, the waiters and cooks. We had some pizza delivered. I doubt they supply milk, for the kids."

"Okay. Our housekeeper in Epsom packed milk for their trip to London. I might get my Head Lad to drive up to collect me to join him for evening stables, and then I'll swing by my house for more milk." A note of irony crept into my voice like a cloud sweeps through an unmarked sky: "If you're not too busy you could show us to our rooms."

The semi-nakedness of his bare, hairy chest no longer seemed to bother the man, but now he was evidently self-conscious about his bare feet. He grabbed a dishcloth and hung it low to cover them. "Certainly, Sir. This way, if you please." With his spare hand he patted his head. His hair was uncombed, still wet from a shower.

I felt I was a New Boy back at Eton in my Housemaster's dreary, cold passages as we formed a crocodile marching through corridor after corridor. We passed two double doors for grand apartments, their carvings ornate with gilded pediments crowning each set of doors, but we ended in what my Dad called "the Bachelors' Rooms." Ours were tacky, with faded draperies and soiled bedspreads, smelling of labradors and the cordite of shotguns. Worse, neither our room nor the childrens' rooms had fires lit in their hearths.

Happy sighed, then went to work. She took our bedspread and shook its dust into the corridor. The childrens' bedspread she folded and deposited in their rooms' one narrow closet. Jeremy had supplied Freddy with the sex but not the ages of our children. Apparently, seven-year-old Timmy was to sleep in a double bed with three-year-old Richard, which meant they would both be wet all night because Richard wasn't housebroken. For five-year-old Dorothy there was a cot suitable for an infant.

Dorothy showed it off with great endearment. "Cot's just right for my Dolly. When you go home for evening stables, will you bring Dolly back with you, for me?"

No contest. I nodded, and swept a light kiss to the top of her curls.

Tentatively, Happy asked: "Could Dorothy sleep with us?"

THAT was not on my list of okays. Rapture in London last night and early this morning! Frustration tonight?

Maybe wet sheets from Dorothy?

No, thank you.

I hugged Happy, and whispered in her left ear that was like a pink shell on some Caribbean shore: "If we are going to have wet sheets, I want them to be wet by you."

Happy grinned, and gave me a thumbs-up. She whispered back: "Nahce if they be wet bah yo-all too."

That did it. I pulled out my iPhone and dialed my Head Lad. I gave him instructions how to find this so-called Ducal Estate, asked him to do me the favor of passing by our cottage to collect bottles of milk and Dorothy's mattress to bring them here, and told him I'd be ready if he alerted me by his mobile when he'd entered the driveway.

Good Old Tom, he did as I'd asked. I turned over the milk and mattress to Happy, who dealt with them appropriately. She'd decided to stay with the kids and forego our evening stables.

Three hours later I returned to the Ducal Estate to find an entirely surrealistic scene. Two lots of arrivals were vieing for the fragile help of Freddy's half-day Daily. Bent over like a broken hoe she balanced cased guns with suitcases for a belligerent paying guest who had headed for the usual quarters he'd had for other shooting parties. The PG was loudly being cursed by overly-outfitted "blue suits" from the United States of America Embassy. Evidently Freddy had simultaneously taken money from Hannibal Kash AND from his usual shooting party PGs.

One harried kennelsman was attempting to control eight labradors on leashes, looking like a fisherman who'd made great catches on eight separate lines. The labradors behaved better than their PG masters.

The Gun House was opened and I viewed an imposing array of Purdies and Holland and Holland shotguns worth altogether about a quarter of a million pounds. Duke Fredddy's estate manager was busily ticketing them with the names of their owners before locking each pair of guns into a series of safes.

Keeping themselves to themselves, outraged that they were being finessed by the PGs of the Duke's shooting party, six members of the Conference struggled up the stairs carrying their Gucci suitcases, lugging them awkwardly to the grander bedrooms.

Happy and my kids, now warmly outfitted in their best and warmest clothes, giggled at the sight of the "blue suits" huffing and puffing on their routes to bedrooms.

Timmy opened the bottle of milk and doled out a glassful to his younger brother and sister. Timmy hated milk, or else he'd have hidden the bottle like an alcoholic to drink it all by himself in private later.

Richard, still too much of an infant to be given a chore, enviously eyed the kennelsman controlling the visiting labradors.

"Yo-all best hurry-up 'n change into yourn night-time clothes. Thet there man wut were na-ked when we'uns arrived, he done put on a mighty special white tie'n long-tailed jacket with satin la-pels signaling thet grown-ups' dinner goin' t'be suhved."

Not half-naked now, the caterers' butler had pre-empted the guests by appearing in what was evidently his uniform for tonight's banquet. I'd been warned by Jeremy to pack my black tie and velvet jacket. Apparently copying old time tradition, this butler would be serving us in a garb worthy of a Ducal hall. What he had not done was to help the new arrivals to find their rooms or deal with their suitcases.

The chaos on the second floor was understandable. Two "blue suits" were stampeding for the same room. The taller of the two won out. Three "blue suits" ended sharing a double room the size of ours. I shrugged, passing their rooms as I hauled Dorothy's mattress to a cot in our sons' room, where it fitted like the filling for a chocolate éclair.

Dinner was another shambles. We hadn't finished the smoked salmon first-course when a tweed-clothed rain soaked PG broke into the formal dining room to shout: "Where the bugger am I supposed to dress, sleep, and shit? Someone's taken my room and en suite toilet."

Freddy, very grand in a midnight blue velvet jacket that might have been his grandfather's, kept seated at the top table and glared at the late arrival.

"Hannibal, you come at this late hour, you can doss down in the nursery wing."

"Damn you, Freddy." The new arrival didn't take that idea as a joke. He grunted, angry as a cat pushed out into rain. He had a European accent I couldn't quite place. "Freddy, you are always hot after that extra sixpence: you invite Americans for a conference here during the best week of the shooting season. So now it's Conference And PGs for a shoot. Lucky I underwrote most of the cost for you. You'd better produce plenty of partridges tomorrow."

The late visitor shouldered his pair of shotguns and grabbed the handle of his battered Louis Vuitton case. This was Hannibal Kash. According to Jeremy Cabrach, Kash is a fore-shortened version of his real name, one which is so famous that he'd been told -- by no less a personality than President Putin -- he must not use it. Jeremy had added that Putin likes this man, and allowed him to make his millions in oil while toeing the party line. I studied him with the probing eye of a surgeon about to operate. Was this grumpy show-off someone I wanted to entrust my wife and her talents to?

When Hannibal returned half an hour later showered and with his unruly hair tidily combed, he was wearing a blue velvet dinner jacket identical to the one Freddy had no doubt found in his castle's attic. I was damned sure this Hannibal Kash hadn't 'found' his velvet jacket. It had the recognizable cut of London's most expensive tailor.

Hannibal's importance at this event was established by Freddy giving him a prominent seat at the top table.

I stared at the second course, duck à l'orange. It lay neatly in the center of a large plate, but it was a very small portion. I put my fork into the meat and thought: "This duck never flew over water. But I'll bet these Americans wouldn't hire a caterer who served up wild duck off a shooting estate, duck that might have pellets that could get caught in guests' cavities." I downed the tasteless spongy meat and glanced along the table to lock eyes with Happy. She was shoveling the second course as if she hadn't eaten all day. But then, she hadn't, had she!

There were no speeches. I reckoned that the Americans were going to sit us down to plenty of those following dinner. One embassy "blue suit", now wearing a tartan tuxedo, gave a short word of thanks to the Duke for providing this venue for the evening's project. I stared at the tartan, and gave a secret laugh: "Too far south of Edinburgh for a tartan." Additional thanks were proffered to Hannibal Kash.

There was no shortage of speeches after coffee and brandy. Ladies were permitted to remain in the dining room, although we were certainly in a most traditional home where it was customary for ladies to have been banished from the male company.

Happy fled up to the childrens' beds to check they were asleep, and missed the most boring speeches. The shooting party guests shuttled off to their rooms, aware the Beaters would be promptly in place for their chance at the pheasants in the first drive at nine a.m.

"I want to welcome our group, and remind everyone to turn off iphones and any other electronic aids to make very sure there are no devices for recording purposes alive in this dining hall," intoned a portly, short, balding embassy "blue suit." He sported a Hitler cropped mustache, which I deemed most inappropriate considering where he worked.

There were clicks and buzzing responses to his request.

He continued: "Forgive me if I keep my opening remarks brief."

I forgave him by speedily heading to the loo. When I returned I found my seat had been taken by Jeremy, who had skipped the dinner. Good grief! He had Fran with him, who was playing the very grand Countess as if she had the lead role in an opera. Aida? No. That's the tale of an Ethiopian Princess.

Jeremy and I were playfully jostling each other's elbows, when the tone that had been so comically light turned as dark as a night sky blackened by an eclipse of the moon.

Hannibal Kash, the shooting party member who'd arrived late, took the microphone from the balding embassy "blue suit."

"I must start by admitting that I do not agree with the President of the United States. That may be painful for some of those present to hear, but I must be truthful when we approach the subject of the many thousands of illegal immigrant children who have been flooding across America's Southern Border. President Obama, who has spoken of an offer of four billion dollars to solve the problem, offers no permanent solution. That will merely enrich lawyers who have to plead the cases of the illegal children."

"Hear, hear!" shouted a Scot, whose Glasgow accent suggested he was no specialist in the plight of illegal immigrant children from places such as Guatemala, Honduras and El Salvador.

The shooting guest continued, lowering his voice while attempting to button his jacket to cover his fat middle: "President Obama's 2012 policy of Deferred Action For Childhood Arrivals has multiplied the problem of children immigrants. The US Congress must stop bickering and allocate funds for these children's crucial necessities. Americans must learn how to ease the immigration process. It must be done in a safe and humane manner, with a new look at the 2008 anti-trafficking law. The Central American nations, which are permitting their children to leave their homelands for perilous journeys across Mexico to reach the American border, must insist on the return of their children and then welcome them home. Mexico should clean up its act and wipe out the Coyotes who get paid to bring these children across the border. On occasion, these same Coyotes rape the girls and boys. Tonight I give you two offers to help stop the flow of illegals. I, personally, propose to pay for the world's greatest dog-handler, a genius at digging out live victims from such as earthquakes, to root out illegals from underground tunnels. Also I have hired one of the brightest of sleuths to track these Coyotes and do away with them."

Applause was sporadic. The embassy "blue suits" were cautious; applause from them was as feeble as raindrops on a desert. Their jobs took them far from America's shores and its Southern Border: they were more interested in doubling their pensions by climbing up the diplomatic ladder.

Jeremy and Fran tapped palms politely, although Fran was quick to stop almost immediately in order to answer the unwelcome ringing of her cellphone. Jeremy, sheepish with embarrassment that she would take a call, refused to lock eyes with me.

The one person who reacted violently was my Happy. She strode into the dining hall glaring like a gladiator in Nero's Roman arena. She'd heard the final part of that over-long not-at-all-brief speech.

"Wur thet fat fella meanin' me? Ah's second to dawgs now?"

Trying to shush her, I took her into my arms and gave her a fervent hug. "What do you care what those "blue suits" think?"

Happy didn't pull away. She wouldn't waste a good hug. "Ah missed eatin' the dessert, only t'come back t'hear me downgraded below a dog-handler! Wut's this whole bus'ness got t'do with us'n anyways?"

Jeremy heard that. "I'll present you to the dog-handler in question and maybe you won't feel so badly."

I put in my tuppence. "Why have the two of you Cabrachs come to this dinner? I thought I was here to be the filler-in for someone. Specifcally, you two."

"You are here because both Harrows are needed. Listen, and you'll understand."

Fran added pompously: "I might take on the Americans' Children Across The Border tragedy as my own personal crusade."

Happy heard that. She'd long ago learned to put a good face on Fran's exaggerations. Then Happy noticed what Fran was wearing and now she smiled warmly at Fran, glad to see there was another woman wearing a short skirt at this formal party. Earlier all the other ladies had appeared in toe-length gowns leaving Happy as poorly kitted out as a sparrow among swans. For all her success at sleuthing, my Happy never changed from being a Kentucky hillbilly. But, her curiosity remained as strong as the day she left those hills for Louisville to learn to be a hot-walker at Churchill Downs.

"Wut all's this Illegal Chillun Across The Southern Border?" Her voice carried far enough to make heads turn. Chairs scraped as bodies swiveled.

"Shut up!" One of the Conference's female secretaries snapped baldly from the row directly ahead. She'd turned in her chair like a snake uncoiling.

Happy shut up.

Now she listened, riveted to her own chair as more speeches described the children's sufferings when sent away from their families.

Specific cases were described of children being sexually abused as they crossed from the southernmost part of Mexico to its unhospitable northern border. Boys raped, girls raped.

Happy was being transformed by what to me were prosaic speeches about a most foreign subject. Of course I'd read for months about the more than fifty thousand children who had crossed into the United States from across the border with Mexico, coming from the poorer nations along Mexico's southern borders.

Some of these kids had come accompanied by a parent or older sibling but most struggled to survive the trip alone.

Happy, who isn't the most assiduous of readers, had learned nothing of this from newspapers, and merely a smattering from TV during our arduous work in Saratoga and in California to rescue the two kidnapped children.

"Fifty seven thousand children crossed our Southern border between October First and June First," droned on a Texan guest who had taken over the microphone.

"Thet man, he got mo'e hairs comin' outta his ears than on his haid," Happy gulped to me, while scribbling the number fifty-seven thousand on the back of a grocery list. "Po'r kiddies, wut they eatin', wheah-all they be sleepin', wut they usin' fo' terlets?"

I answered her in a whisper that brought more heads swiveling our way. "Once they've crossed the border, most are taken to containment centers waiting for a turn before a judge who will decide if each specific child gets returned across the border. Next, with luck, the child is granted a chance to be brought before an immigration court to rule on a future in the U.S.A."

"How long do thet take?"

"Could be years."

"Rick! Thet be turrible! Could we adopt one o' them kids?"

"No chance. Usually any kid who makes the journey across Mexico into the United States hopes a relative will be waiting. Maybe a parent, grandparent, uncle or aunt. And those who can go to a relative have a better case for staying in the U.S.A."

Happy scribbled that information on another page of her grocery list. For a few moments she listened attentively, again, when Hannibal Kash returned to the microphone. The shooting party guest had more to say.

"I came here to present a plan. I will fund it. And I will do all in my power to make it work. I've already outlined what must be done. Let's get to it; let's trap those Coyotes and skin them."

Jeremy touched my right elbow. "That's the Big Man of the Night. HE is underwriting this Conference, not the U.S. Embassy. Any of the Diplomats who came were on his agenda. Our MI6 people are interested in his project because we've been tracking some of the Coyotes involved."

"Coyotes?"

"Coyotes are what they've named the human traffickers in this business. Coyotes. Some used to be drug dealers, or worked for drug dealers. When marijuana was legalized in states of the U.S., the Coyotes decided there was more sure money in offering to get illegals across the U.S. Southern border. Charge about $7,000 per person. Not a lot of money to them, but considering the scale of this business, it has attracted the evils."

Fran added: "A parent of a child, endangered by the drug wars or political infighting in one of those Central American countries, somehow manages to scrape up the $7,000. The chappie on the microphone, Hannibal Kash, is dedicating his considerable fortune to do what he can to wipe out these Coyotes."

"He must have a lot of money."

"Yes. He does. Hannibal has offered to recruit doctors, nurses, psychiatrists and such to provide medical assistance to those children who need it. Seems that there are children who have been sent to the U.S.A. with health issues in hopes they will be cured there. Tuberculosis, polio, mental disorders, you name it, they bring their diseases with them."

I asked very specifically: "Jeremy, why is Happy here? I heard Hannibal Kash say he's hired a top sleuth. Does he mean my Happy? First we'd heard about it."

"You, of all people, haven't figured that out?"

"Yes, now that you mention those Coyotes. But we're a long way from Mexico."

Jeremy, who was usually so parsomonious with his grins, gave me a huge smile. He delved into an inner pocket of his velvet jacket to extract two airline tickets. "For you and Happy. Non-stop to Mexico

City. And return. Happy's job comes with excellent pay, bonuses, and all incidentals included."

"Happy's job!"

"You will be Sancho Panza to her feminine version of Don Quixote. But you're on the payroll, too."

Now I took an in-depth look at the evening's main speaker. He was middle-aged, with the paunch, thinning hair, and veined nose that often come from too many banquets and drinks parties. Short, not much taller than Happy, he had small hands. I couldn't see his feet. But I reckoned he wasn't a man with the big feet of a sensual person, because he was centering all his passion on this business of kids crossing the U.S. border.

His eyes sent signals out to Happy in a way that made me think of rocket launchers. I imagined he could make a loyal friend but a God-awful enemy.

Hannibal Kash ended with a moving plea for help.

No checkbooks appeared. The embassy people had been avalanched with information regarding the border crisis. None of those present were involved in financing projects.

I tapped Jeremy's elbow. "Introduce me," I suggested. "I want to get to him before he gets to Happy."

"No deal?"

"No. Happy has her hands full with our own kids."

"She managed somehow in California, ending those kidnappings According to the PRIVATE EYE article about her, she wiped out a serious onset of trafficking for illegal adoptions."

"Our wonderful Nanny held the fort for Happy with our children. She's due for a vacation."

"Her vacation will have to be put on hold. Come on, I'll introduce you to Hannibal You can talk to him while Happy meets the dog-handler."

Chapter 3

One week later we were on that non-stop to Mexico City. Happy had agreed to Hannibal Kash's offer. She'd felt deeply touched by the plight of illegal Central American children traveling on average two thousand miles alone to Mexico's northern border. A Nanny had been hired by Kash to nanny our children's Nanny.

Funds from Hannibal flowed as if from the coffers of the Koch twins, one of whom is on the Forbes List numbered at the seventh richest man in the U.S.A.

I don't know where or on which global list Hannibal ranks, but it can't be far beyond judging from the way Hannibal was underwriting events to draw further attention to the children-crossing-the-border crisis.

He certainly wanted to keep interest in it alive with America's bleeding-hearts housewives, until the US Government ante-ed up the billions President Obama had asked for from Congress.

On a telephone call Happy received at Heathrow Airport, he boasted: "Daily now, I have a PR firm feeding all of America's top TV stations and newspapers the newest crimes against these children. Yesterday, a six-year-old illegal died of hypothermia on the Mexico side, opposite the Nevada desert. Another kid took a photo of the corpse with his iPhone and put it on the internet.'

"Oh, golly!" Happy had difficulty breathing into her iPhone.

In a darker tone, Hannibal added: "And here is some news you may or may not want to hear: the dog-handler whom I had hoped to hire, he has sent apologies. He had to fly to India, where an entire town, hit be an earthquake, is in ruins with live people trapped under the fallen buildings. Our handler friend has left for Delhi followed by a huge amount of publicity. Personally, I fear that too much is hoped-for from his dog."

"Gee," Happy tried again to breathe, but her voice came out as a wheeze. "Ah wuz lookin' fo'ward to meetin' his dog Rex."

Not realizing she'd be cutting short their conversation, Happy clicked shut her iPhone. She went to a newspaper shop and chose the New York Times to look for any write-up about *our* trip to Mexico. No PR to advertise the Harrows' two jobs! Happy and I were in an opposite scenario from the handler's dog, Rex. *His trip to India had been featured.* No one was to know what kind of pilgrimage we were on, with the exception of those "blue suits," and members of the Duke's shooting party who were at the Oxfordshire dinner.

Within nine hours we were flying over Mexico's City's Sleeping Woman Volcano, Popocatapetl, our airplane grazing its peaks in a foolhardy plunge by our pilot that the airline execs would must certainly have disapproved of.

Arriving at Mexico City's airport, Happy groaned, "Ah sho' re-membuhs this here place. Ah caint fo'get how Guadalupe sent a selfie of huh female parts to thet Frenchie who weren't much mo'e than a gigolo. Ah re-membuhs how she done disappeahed into the Ladies Terlets to take thet selfie. Sho hopes this-here visit will be less friv'lous."

Happy shouldn't have given that selfie memory so much thought. Bad elves must have heard her, because this trip started out in a way that was anything but frivolous.

We were chloroformed and thrown into a garbage dump within minutes of our arrival. Identified and targeted as we stood in line for a taxi, unthinkingly we'd boarded a black taxi that had swerved up ahead of the queue, its driver leaning from his seat to open its rear door for us.

At the first stop light leaving the airport's premises, two armed gang members had jumped aboard through the opposite rear door. I was hit by a left and a right. Downed, immobile on the taxi's grimy floor. Happy had her breath knocked out by a hard push into a corner. Then we were both chloroformed.

We woke up lying among empty bottles and stinking garbage in a far barrio's abandoned lot. Happy's new and very expensive camera – a gift from Hannibal – was missing, as was her iPhone, but her handbag topped a pile of empty cans not far from where we lay. My British passport was gone along with all of Hannibal's Midas-size cash allowance. I searched my undershirt for the hidden tuck where I'd stashed my credit card. That, at least, was there.

Happy spoke first. "Don't lets usn tell the chillun 'bout this. They'd worry."

"Here, let me help you get up." I put a hand on my right knee and raised myself out of the filth before giving a hand to help Happy. We looked at each other, our shoulders sank, and then we laughed, hard.

"Yo-all got any money left? Ah thinks us'n got ournselves mugged."

"No. No money. Not a farthing. And no, we weren't mugged. Targeted. This was a Mexico 'hola' to warn us to behave ourselves. The Coyotes know we're here. And they want us to know they don't like it."

"Ah's got coupla dolluhs. Think a bus drivuh will ac-cept US curr'ncy?"

"Worth a try, if we can find a bus."

"Yo-all heah wut Ah heahs? Be lahke a fair beyond yonder trees. Let's usn go see."

The so-familiar tune of BESAME MUCHO lilted over the poor landscaping of a park beyond. We made our way out of the lot's garbage, picking off bits of old orange peel and chunks of serious filth, to cross the park opposite and arrive at a busy street-market. The music came from loudspeakers, the din came from the vendors shouting out their wares.

Happy counted out her few dollars. She went to a T-shirt stall and wrangled for a pair of shirts. She found a tent where jeans were on offer with a cubicle to try them for size. She paid for two pairs, and we took the stalls modestly lettered *Hombres Mujeres*.

Emerging from my cubicle, now kitted out in the new T-shirt and jeans, I saw Happy hurrying toward the bus stop where a partly-filled bus had jerked its brakes.

"Hurry, Rick-Honey. This be fahne." Happy had squeezed between a cook with an angry live duck and a butler carrying a load of kitchen pans. The three were at the end of a queue of early domestics who had already made their purchases.

I joined Happy who was skillfully warding off the duck's vicious snapping. Dumb duck! He couldn't best my Happy, who'd disciplined many a racehorse.

Happy waved two dollar-bills at the bus driver. "yo-all ac-cept Uni-ted States money?" she asked, as we climbed aboard.

No verbal reply. The driver wordlessly placed the dollar bills in his pants' pocket.

"Any idea where this bus is headed?" I queried,

"Sho do. We's goin; t'Elga's barrio. See the sign?"

I saw and I remembered what had once been a fancy 'barrio.' "We're to be guests of Elga, with her orangutan?"

"Yup."

In a raucous voice, like a macaw's, she welcomed me in what had once been a clipped British accent now muddied with a trans-Atlantic drawl: "Positively lovely to see you, Rick. What a joy to have you two dears to visit! No suitcases? I should certainly want you to stay a good while."

Behind Elga lurked her orangutan, Marta.

"I see you still have Marta." I tried to show some warmth.

Our frail, blue-dyed-hair hostess tried to straighten her widow's hump, and said gently: "Dear, dear Rick. But of course I have. We've been a twosome for over seventeen years. She was my present to myself on my seventy-third birthday. Come along, Martica. Say welcome to Rick and Happy."

Marta was well schooled. She didn't try to shake hands. Lucky for us. I'd heard that Marta had broken both of Elga's arms several times. Marta swirled her lips like a wine-taster, jumped up and down twice, then settled and returned to her lurking posture.

Elga said, "You want a whisky. Come along inside and tell me what you plan to do while in Mejico."

"Happy's under contract to put her know-how to use in this enormous problem of Central American kids crossing illegally to the U.S.A. We've just cracked a kidnapping case in California where child traffickers were as numerous as ants on an abandoned hill. I'm being paid to act as Happy's back-up."

"Terrible the way rich childless elderly folk support a kidnapping business to get a child. Also there are many young women who want to save their figures and skip childbirth. Rick, let me top up your glass. Yes, and what's Happy drinking?"

Happy had found a can of coca cola in the fridge. She drank straight from the can, until Elga slipped a hand-cut crystal glass on to the kitchen's hospitality island. Elga said forcefully, yet in a courteous way: "Don't offer coca cola to Martica. I have her on a strict diet."

"What's her favorite food?"

"Orange sherbert. We will go for a drive and get some in a minute. First, I want to know why you are dressed in T-shirts and jeans. With flip flops for shoes!"

Happy took a huge slug of her drink. "Ma'am, we'uns got mugged first stop-light beyond thet airpo't. Chlo'fomed, we been-thrown into a garbage dump, our'n suitcases stolen. Rick's passpo't 'n money too. Ah'd stuffed some dollahs down into mah bra. 'Nuf to take a bus to yo-all."

"I don't believe we were mugged. Targeted, that yes. And Happy didn't mention that what the crooks didn't take were our return tickets. That sent me a message."

"How dreadful!" Elga belonged to a past generation that didn't use swear words.

We were led into the formal drawing room. There, I felt I'd returned to my grandmother's flat on Eaton Square, which my father sold when she passed on in order to buy that useless group of farms in Warwickshire that never earned a farthing. Elga had brought to Mexico her George II chairs with their straight legs, a George III table with its rounded knees, an Eighteenth Century Aubusson rug and a Louis IV sofa topped by a painting of a Restoration belle.

Marta jumped up and down to draw Elga's attention. With her fingered paws she made a twelve inch diameter circle, in their sign language.

Elga left the drawing room hurriedly. To Marta, she signed "You made the driving wheel circle. We will leave now. Open the garage door." We were duly informed that Marta is very handy with locks and she loves to deal with that garage door.

Parked in the garage, a 1956 blue Bentley filled the narrow parking space. This garage had been built when gas prices rose, convincing the general public that smaller vehicles were preferable.

Marta, wearing a diaper, took what was obviously her usual place on the back seat. There was a ready thick towel over half a sheet of plastic to protect the Bentley's red leather. Happy, trying not to shriek, climbed in beside Marta. I took the front passenger seat next to Elga.

The Bentley had a right-hand drive. "My late husband bought this car," Elga whispered. "I shipped it from Oxfordshire to Miami after he died, when I believed I would move there. Martica has always known this automobile."

While Elga warmed up the motor, I asked: "Excuse me, but would it be all right if you would take me to the British Embassy, before you get sherbets?"

"Certainly, Rick. I had it in mind to suggest that. Only I'm not that familiar with the streets to get there. I go to the British Embassy Residence to parties, but I haven't had a need to go the offices."

God! Elga proceeded to prove just how unfamiliar she was with the streets. She almost mowed down a wedding party, the bride in a marshmallow-shaped gown accompanied by her vast family all the ladies kitted out in extravagant dresses with matching hats.

The hats went flying.

Happy, who some years earlier had been obsessed by classical buildings, managed to see the Cathedral before Elga's erratic driving shut out that view.

"It be market day," Happy said, pointing out peons who had come into the capital to sell corn, mangoes, or whatever.

Chapter 4

These farm folk didn't wear the short knee-length trousers of years ago and their china poblanas didn't wear full embroidered skirts like what you'd see on tourism adverts. Almost all of them were in the same type of T-shirts and jeans Happy and I had bought.

I was speculating on what those snobbish embassy employees would think of my kit. At least it would indicate there was truth to my story of having been chloroformed and dumped into garbage. The clothes I'd traveled in had been what I wore at home as a racehorse trainer, a corduroy jacket and grey slacks.

Hovering in front of a red light, her ready foot on the accelerator, Elga asked: "What about Happy? Doesn't she need to go to HER embassy?"

"Elga, that's a sore point. I list her on my passport, she has dual nationality, so for the time being I prefer she doesn't alert those 'blue suits' at the US Embassy. SOMEONE made a call to the top Coyote, which is why we were what Happy calls 'mugged.' Why don't you two go shopping? She can't stay forever in what she's wearing now. I'm going to have the embassy help me establish my identity at Barclays Bank to get money. Meanwhile, could you lend her some?"

Elga had to save the Bentley from a nasty scraping. Shaken, she altered her tone, upping it an octave. "Big fancy car that was going to collide with us. Expensive car. Maybe belongs to a Coyote. They go for fancy cars." Changing to her normal quiet tone, she added: "Yes, I can certainly lend Happy whatever amount she needs. And I know an adorable shop that belongs to a friend who breeds ocelots on her hacienda grounds. Loves her ocelots like I love Martica. What a thrill

I got the first time I heard her ocelots purr. They are felines, you know. Somewhat like leopards."

My first stop was the embassy offices. Identification was made, help given.

Meanwhile Marta had been off-loaded from the Bentley at Elga's friend's shop. Marta looked very pleased to be in the shop, doing a jumping-for-joy act. She recognized a welcome when she got one. Like a dwarf, or a crippled handicapped person, Marta knew that her appearance was held against her. There were people in Mexico City who thought an orangutan should not live in their city.

Happy tried on several dresses. They were suitable for elderly ladies, not Happy's taste. She chose beige silk slacks with a rose silk blouse, topped by a long jacket cut like a doctor's medical tunic.

"Now for Martica's orange sherbet." Again Elga selected a shop where Marta's presence wouldn't provoke a wild scramble from other paying customers. And again, Marta looked supremely pleased.

Happy began to understand what Elga was doing with her orangutan. "Tell me, Elga, how'd yo-all find Marta. What made yo'all share yourn life with huh?"

"It's quite a story," Elga licked her chocolate ice cream like a kid at a fair, "One evening in Miami, watching TV, I saw a documentary about a sad ex-laboratory orangutan that had been banished from his university scientists to live in a zoo. A male, for quite some years he had enjoyed the life of a student, learning sign language. His photograph was in the University of Tennessee yearbook. He had been housed in a trailer on the campus grounds, roamed freely, and was driven weekly to his favorite drive-in ice cream parlor. But when a new President arrived at the University, he declared this orangutan was a menace and must be sent to a zoo. Now here comes the horrible part. While waiting to go to the zoo, this orangutan was stuck in a five foot by five foot cage in a quarantine facility before being transferred. By the time he went to the zoo the poor creature was deeply traumatized. No one to communicate with by sign language. No ice cream parlors. He fell Into a deep depression. I resolved to go see him. And did. The day I went, one of the scientists who had reared him, called Lyn, was visiting. It was heart wrenching to watch their forbidden reunion, the two not permitted to come closer to each other than any tourist. I made up my mind to give another orangutan a chance. Hence, Martica."

Elga had arrived at her barrio. Suddenly she tensed.

"Anythin' the mattuh?"

"Happy, hide. Quickly. Put your head down. I don't like the look of that Maserati careening in front of my house. Ladies and gentlemen from my quarter do not drive Maseratis. Hide! I think the chauffeur is looking for you!"

Happy got far down in the back, without disturbing Marta.

Elga pulled up in front of a neighboring house. It was a brothel. "This place belongs to a woman from Mississippi, who has always run brothels. She has a kind heart. Get out quickly. Tell her you want work. I will let you know when this Maserati leaves."

There was a back entrance to the brothel from its garage. Cheating husbands used it to clandestinely park their cars. Shaken, Happy found a bell and rang it. The brothel's madam answered. At first she looked delighted, thinking she had an early customer, but at a second look at Happy who walks like a jockey, she barked in a Deep South accent: "We-all don't do lesbians heah."

Happy recognized a home-country accent. "Ain't lookin' fo' one. Ah needs a hidin' place. Yo-all willin' t'help a good Kentucky gal?"

"De-pends. Ah's not wantin' no trouble with the po-lice. Drugs? Beat up a guy, left him fo' daid?"

"Nah. Nothin' lahke thet. Ah's heah in Mexico t'help them Central 'Merican kids wut go crossin' the 'Merican border. Please, just a li'l while 'till mah husband come fo' me."

The Madam jerked her head to motion Happy to climb a flight of red-carpeted steps. Happy emerged into a large parlor also fitted in red. Red carpet, red curtains, red sofas and chairs. There were -naked girls of various types on the sofas. Among the girls were blonde Russians, burly Germans, two African-Americans and three busty Mexicans.

A Russian woman was called over by the Madam and introduced to Happy. "This be someone from the Uni-ted States. Don't know nothin' about huh. Irina, yo'all speaks English. Take huh up to the in-firm'ry."

Together with Irina, Happy managed another flight of red-carpeted steps. She emerged into a spotless, highly sanitized chamber with a gynecologist's table that featured stirrups. There were two sets of facing cots. Two night tables with an alarm clock and a bottle of Nestlé water on each. One chair: no visitors were likely to be permitted here.

"Ah's bin t'Russia," Happy opened a conversation, trying to be friendly.

Irina, like a mud puddle that was ugly unless transformed by reflecting a gorgeous sunset, gave a smile that turned her into a beautiful woman. Previously she had been miserly with any sort of pleasant expression. Happy's outgoing offer of friendship had transformed her. But she responded strangely to this show of warmth. She wrinkled her nose like a child encountering a puppy, wondering if it would bite.

Creasing her wrinkles, she said: "I, too, have been to your country. But do not speak of Russia as my country. I despise memories of my childhood, young adulthood. Will you believe that I once worked for what was then known as the KGB? But my face became too well-known. It was no longer convenient for me to be alive. I, too, had to hide. A friend suggested a brothel would be clever place to hide. But not brothel in the United States or in Russia."

"All Ah's seen in Russia were hossraces. Yo'all got some maghty fine hosses."

"I have never been to a horse race. I was a night girl. The day women went to horse races."

"Ah's been in coupl'a Russ-ian ho-tels. Not enny fa-mous ones. 'N mostly in their bahs. Mah hus-band, he be a hoss trainuh, always lookin' fo' customuhs o' tryin' t'please one. So's he takes 'em to bahs."

"I cannot go to bars. I cannot be seen outside of this place."

"Well, we'uns got thet in common. Hey, Ah heahs the bell. Could it be mah husband?"

Irina peered out of the infirmary's one window. "Nyet. Just a John looking for a bit of fun. Fun! *Spa siva*, when you go to wherever it is you are going, if it is in a solitary place, please you will take me with you. I hate this brothel life. Safe, maybe. But nyet, I cannot any more this take."

Happy was reminded of Elga's story about the Tennessee zoo orangutan. Safe, but it was a terrible life.

The second time the bell rang Irina announced: "This time your husband it is."

"RICK'S mah life. Listen up, gonna go now. But Ah's gonna remembuh wut yo-all done offered."

Happy galloped down the stairs to the garage door, like a two-year-old filly in a maiden race. She came through the exit's trick door.

She clung to me as if we'd been parted for years. "Turrible place, this. Ain't gonna give no goodbye to thet Miss'sippi woman. Be it safe now at Elga's?"

"Darling, I'm not sure." I was wearing my just-bought blue suit. "We're invited for dinner at the British Embassy Residence. Elga's ready to drive us there, knows the way well. You've got to change into whatever you've acquired during your shopping spree."

Crestfallen, Happy hugged my arm, wailing, "Ah's bought PANTS. Trousers. Slacks, yo-all knows wut Ah means. Ah cain't go to no embassy dinner in pants. Yo-all go on yourn own."

Marta unlocked Elga's garage door.

Elga was waiting for us, her face alight. "Embassy dinner! How heavenly. Wish I was invited. Happy darling, you must hurry and change. Cannot be late to a British Embassy dinner." In her arms she carried what to me looked like an ancient altar cloth. "Dear Happy, I am going to lend you what I wore to my first embassy dinner."

I watched Happy swallow, the veins of her neck bulging. That's a familiar sign that she feels upset, but didn't want to make others suffer. "Thankee, Elga. Let me try it on."

Unfortunately for Happy, the damned velvet skirt fit.

With a matching tired velvet handbag, Happy climbed into the Bentley's rear seat alongside Marta, busily attempting to keep the orangutan's fingered paws from grabbing the bottom of the skirt to peer upward.

The British Embassy was well fortified. A smartly uniformed guard gave us both a feeling of safety, like a good Nanny soothing children afraid of a dark night.

Other arriving guests stared at Elga and her Bentley, with its seated orangutan. Elga waved grandly, with a Queen's acknowledgement of the crowd beyond. Wonderful Elga, she hadn't been fazed by the Jackal in her road that afternoon. She wasn't unnerved by staring fellow Britishers.

Well-dressed guests looking down their noses weren't going to make HER feel put down.

I watched Elga change gears and speed away, and wondered what this dinner could bring to equal her hospitality.

The dinner proved to be a delight. Everything about it was exquisitely managed. Staff knew exactly what to do. Houseguests complimented Happy on her new blouse. Nobody sent sneering looks at her dilapidated skirt. The subject of Central American children illegally crossing the US border was tactfully evaded. Happy's winning a horse race in Tokyo was extolled, my Arkansas Derby win was mentioned.

Two guests, a married couple -- Colonel and Mrs. Wyatt -- offered to drive us to Elga's house. It could have proved a perfect evening, reminiscent of others I'd once enjoyed as a Deb's Delight after leaving Eton. But the evening turned ominous when we entered Elga's road.

A Maserati lurked within ten feet of her garage.

There were no welcoming lights on in Elga's house. A warning! Stay away! Get away! Make tracks!

Very quietly, Happy said to Colonel Wyatt, "Puhlease tu'n back. Ah's fo'gotten mah handbag. Could yo-all puhlease take us back to the embassy?"

Colonel Wyatt sensed the urgency like a good hound of the Warwickshire hunt scents trouble. He recognized there was a threat in that Maserati. He reversed without drawing attention, while Happy crouched low.

She was welcomed back to the embassy, although all the other guests had left. There, we thanked Colonel and Mrs. Wyatt, gave excuses to Ambassador and Mrs. Duncan Taylor, asked for a taxi, and went straight to Mexico City's main bus terminal.

Bus terminals serviced all the far flung states of this mountainous country. This, however, was THE terminal for Central American hopefuls on their way to the American border.

Didn't I recall how bad some of Mexico's roads were? Hadn't I only recently needed to walk for miles to safety with a prize racehorse to get away from a gangster who had stolen it from Guadalupe?

I bought two tickets for Ciudad Juarez, on the Mexico-El Paso border. The next bus was not due to leave for five hours.

"Rick-Honey, Ah's got an idee how we-uns c'n git ourn sens'ble clothes from Elga's. Ah's got huh 'phone numbuh. Ah's gonna ask huh to drive mah new friend Irina t'this heah bus tuminal with ourn jeans, flip flops, mah 'Merican passpoht, 'n ourn re-tuhn tickets t'England. Irina c'n re-tuhn this heah handbag 'n skirt t'Elga."

"Why this Irina? Who is this woman? Some prostitute you met in the brothel? Come on, my darling. Why an Irina when Elga can deal with our things?"

I dreaded her reply. God, how well I knew how Happy can befriend people who are seriously undesirable.

"Irina, she be Russ-ian."

"Yes, I gathered that from the name."

"Soviet Russ-ian. Used to work fo' thet KGB. Face got too well-known. She were goin' t'be – wut she done call it -- exPENdable. Hahdin' in thet theah brothel. Hated it. Ah mo'e less done tol' huh we'd take huh with usn when we left town. Ah thinks she c'd be maghty use-ful."

No arguing with Happy. I learned years ago to say "Yes, Dear." Hence, our blissful marriage.

Elga deposited Irina with us within a half an hour. She brought our jeans, T-shirts and flip flops; and more importantly, our return tickets to Britain, should we live to use them.

Irina looked very different from when she escorted Happy to the brothel's garage-door. She'd washed the brash platinum highlights from her hair, changed into jeans and a T-shirt, and amazingly changed her dour depressed facial expression to one of purpose and resolve.

"Thankee for ever'thin'. Ah loves yo-all," Happy gulped to Elga, both on the verge of tears.

"Now don't make me cry. I won't be able to drive the Bentley," Elga droned. "I can't stay here for long. I left Martica back at the house, asleep. I don't like to change her routine, you know."

I saw Elga to the terminal's parking lot. More calmly, Elga said a gloomy goodbye to me: "Keep your Happy safe," she said, nodding at Happy who was waving to her from the terminal, tears now being gulped into her mouth. Happy appeared so forlorn, like a first time boarding school newcomer being left at a forbidding dormitory. "She's heading for more trouble than she knows."

Chapter 5

Irina proved useful from the first hour. She knew well how to make us invisible.

In a nearly-empty terminal during its quietest time of night, Irina located three seats in a row semi-occupied by peons and china poblanas, all with serapes covering their faces to shield them from florescent lights.

She found the stall selling serapes. Bought three. Gave us two. Settled herself near us with her serape over her face. I showed Happy how to most efficiently place her serape to hide her head and white neck. And to get relief from the stink of perspiration, urine, and unwashed jeans emanating from the peons.

I finally got two hours of rest.

It was five a.m. when Irina's professionally probing hand found my right shoulder. I recognized Irina's personal odors of perspiration and female parts, slid down the serape and saw Irina gesturing toward new arrivals: very quiet children between the ages of seven and eleven. They came unescorted, timidly, with heavy-lidded eyes and tired clothes. Both carried bus tickets.

Happy woke up, took in the meaningful scene, tapped her lips to warn me not to speak, and made for toilets marked SEÑORAS.

Irina followed Happy, but did not enter a cubicle. Two of the young girls had followed them into the washroom and were diligently quitting layers of dust and mud. They were't talking in Spanish. They were wearing the perennial T-shirt and jeans. But their hair, braided to their waists, gave away their Guatemalan nationality. Braids had gone out of fashion with Mexican girls, many of whom had dyed their hair blond and teased their indian straight locks into undulating waves.

Irina knocked on Happy's cubicle door. Happy emerged to hear Irina whisper: "Children not Mexican. Guatemalan. Their language unfamiliar, but in KGB I learned to recognize less known local dialects. This is Guatemalan Mayan. Nalga."

Irina spoke to the elder girl in Spanish. "Ustedes vienen de Ciudad de Guatemala? Van a Tejas?"

Two terrified expressions waved over their faces like tiny tsunamis. No reply.

Happy noticed a septic sore on the younger child's bare arm. She gestured to it, and with her most motherly smile offered to dress it. Slowly, very gently, Happy washed the sore with water from a basin's tap. She drew a band-aid from her purse, expertly applied its bandage to the middle section of the silent girl's brown arm, pushed down on the adhesive, and gave an even wider smile.

"Nyet, this is not convenient," Irina scolded. "Girl needs be tested. Her sore could be contagious."

"Po'r li'l tyke. Could be mah own Dorothy! Wish Ah'd some pen'cillin ointment fo' huh."

"Much penicillin and other anti-biotics needed for this child."

"Watcha think? These heah kids could be met by one o' them Coyotes at the other end o' ourn bus ride?"

"Almost certainly."

When the two Guatemalan girls left the washroom, Irina splashed water under both her arms, where she had heavy unshaven bushes. She also washed the bush between her legs. Two hours in the over-heated terminal had brought out a womanly stink.

She frowned as she dried herself with paper towels: "Safer we take another bus. Girls bring trouble."

"Nah. Ah thinks we be smaht t'git a looksee if a Coyote do come. Ain't gonna be no high-up Coyote. Low on t'ladduh when sent t'collect two kids from a bus sta-tion."

Happy returned from the "terlets" to whisper: "Rick-Honey, Ah reckons we got usn some o' them re-fu-gee kids on ourn bus."

I said. "Yes. I figured that. I saw them go into the toilets. We'd best take a later –"

"Nah. Let's usn learn us how this op'ration works."

We were the first to board, to be able to go as far in the rear as possible. We watched as a last-minute group of hopeful illegals took front seats. The lead girl, an eleven-year-old, handed the groups' tickets to the bus driver. She got a flirtatious up-and-down from the driver. He'd been surly and possibly about to refuse entry to the kids, but after a thorough look at her, he smacked his lips like a boy eating cotton candy. Nodding his head, he accepted the envelope after shoving his hairy hand toward the crease in her jeans. He liked what he felt. He grinned, showing that he missed a front tooth. He waved the envelope. He guessed, and we guessed, that it contained a suitably sized tip.

Hours and hours passed. The bus climbed up mountain peaks, its radiator steaming. It plunged precipitously into tepid valleys. We felt unbearably hot, then unbearably cold, then hot again depending whether we cruised at lowland levels or rose to high altitudes.

There were a few rest-and-recreation stops. At the last stop before Ciudad Juarez the eleven-year-old lead girl was pushed into an available shed by the bus driver to add rape to his booty. She emerged weeping fifteen minutes later.

I observed this episode.

Thankfully my Happy missed it because she'd been too busy buying tacos for the two she'd met in Mexico City. Lucky! Happy would surely have drawn attention to us by attacking the bus driver. Most certainly she'd have attacked him. If she'd had a jockey's whip with her she'd have left permanent scars on his face and neck.

I'd decided not to take on the bus driver. I could have given him a good beating with my fists alone: I was six inches taller and fifty pounds lighter. But Happy and I were on a job, one that entailed observing this type of criminal behavior without causing an incident.

The rest-and-recreation stop added a new contingent of refugees. As this was the last of these stops before our arrival at a Border Town, these new arrivals had probably flown in by airplane but were hopeful that by backtracking to arrive by bus, they could pass for locals.

God, this was some busload: all of us hoping to avoid detection!

Chapter 6

At the bus terminal of a Ciudad Juarez suburb we saw our first Coyote; a tall, heavy-set , swarthy man I nicknamed Homburg hat because of his last century headgear.

Homburg hat wasn't looking our way. He was too busy collecting envelopes, with their cash. He wasn't going to interest himself in any passengers who didn't offer an envelope. Two hopeful illegals jostled to get to the head of the queue to finalize their trip to the U.S.A., flashing money without bothering about any envelope. As nimble as a dancer Homburg hat grabbed their cash before any other Coyote could stop him.

Three girls were left behind when all the other hopeful illegals took to the road with the Coyotes.

In Oxfordshire, when giving us instructions, Jeremy and Hannibal had provided Happy with a map detailing the most often used routes into Ciudad Juarez. I studied it now and recognized which one would be implemented today.

It was the easiest of the routes.

Why had three girls been left behind? I recognized the eleven-year-old girl who had been raped by the bus driver. Her hair and skirt were still disheveled. The other two girls were the two Happy had befriended.

Happy didn't delay in offering help to her two small friends.

"C'mon, yo-all," she herded them to a clump of very dry mescal.

Peyote cactus doesn't provide cover, but a wholly unexpected taxi stand nearby offered shade. While we huddled away from the sizzling sunshine, the eleven-year-old rape victim painfully came over ro join us. Ashamed of the dried blood on her legs, she tried to shove them as far as possible under her ripped skirt. But we could see that between them blood still oozed to trickle down to her ankles.

"Po'r li'l thing, she look so 'shamed. Weren't none o' hern doin'. T'were thet filthy drivah wut were criminal." As she spoke, a taxi's horn bleated. It swerved to a full stop in front of Happy, its driver obviously hungry for a fare. "C'mon l'l gal," she said to the child rape victim. "Ah's takin' yo-all t'hos-pi-tal fo' a nec'ssary clean-out."

Hospital!

Great idea! Happy always came up trumps. While Irina translated Happy's suggestion to the pre-teenage victim, I packed our growing group into the taxi's ample rear.

The claptrap taxi had a woman driver. Middle aged, she adopted a sympathetic expression, obviously feeling pity for the three girls. She'd seen thousands just like them, but had never had cause to invite any of them into her taxi. In fractured English, she introduced herself: "I call me Odilia. Like old saint."

The two little girls sat in front with Odilia. There was no way Happy could have got the eleven-year-old to return to sit with a driver, even a female driver. She huddled between Irina and Happy, tears beginning at last to flow. I was odd man out, perched on a jump seat.

"Ah's thinkin' a HOS-PI-TAL not a bad place fo' usn t'hang out. None o' them Coyotes come lookin' fo' usn in a hos-pi-tal."

I might have disagreed when I took a thorough look at the hospital chosen by Odilia. It was small and slightly dilapidated. Had she chosen it because the fare was increased by its distant location? It most certainly was NOT on the most convenient route into Ciudad Juarez.

The place was as forlorn as the graveyards where many of its patients had ended. From its peeling Spanish Colonial Style façade to the leaning Byzantine cross on its Pisa-like tower, there was evidence of an urgent need of funding. I guessed it had been built long before Mexico's communist era of the 1930s. The gracious architectural features, its arches, the façade's swirling lines, a romanesque doorway and the pillared hall certainly belonged to a long ago time. So did the nun who welcomed us wearing a complicated ankle-length black habit with a huge starched, white wimple hiding her cropped hair.

I'd read that nuns no longer wore habits, but appeared in clothes suitable for any modest woman. Apparently, in this far-flung border area, that news had yet to arrive.

"I am Mother Antonia. And who is the patient?" She spoke in hesitant but correct English.

Happy, whose use of the English language was sorely in need of improvement, had never seen a nun in this passé regalia. She curtseyed, as if to The Queen. For a moment my Happy looked as gauche as a new girl joining a kindergarten.

"How do you do, Mother," I took over to deal with the niceties, while Happy proceeded to calm the victimized eleven-year-old who was now gasping for air between violent throes of weeping.

Groping for the appropriate wording, I stumbled over the subject of rape. How not to offend this old-fashioned nun?

Our formerly brothel-based companion, Irina, had no such concern. Like a Miura bull entering the Plaza de Toros, she rushed to the fray. "*Kak ve*, nun, look at the blood on this girl's skirt. Bus driver raped her. She needs sedative, washing out with vaginal douche, good dose of antibiotics."

Ignoring Irina's bluntness, Mother Antonia placed a soothing arm around the eleven-year-old. In Spanish. she cooed gently: "Bienvenida, m'hija. You are very welcome here. We have seen this before, you are not the first to suffer such brutality. Tell me child, what is your name?"

That question was based on solid experience on how to create an opening.

The girl had met nuns before. Trained in her home village's convent school to always show respect for the religious, she reined in her weeping like a good jockey controls a mount. She gasped: "Maria. Please, I must go to Confession, Mother. I have –"

"No child, we leave the Sacraments until tomorrow morning's Mass. And I feel sure you have nothing to confess. Whatever happened was in no way YOUR fault. Now you must eat something. Do you like tamales?"

Without any more palaver with the three adults, she led the three girls to an ornate dining hall. Two nuns served all three children from a fresh platter of tamales, while I tried to lure Mother Antonia into the possibility of granting over-night hospitality to the girls. "Would it be possible for the three girls to stay with you? I am certain they are dehydrated, and possibly have been exposed to rotten food. Also my wife and I, and our traveling companion, need a place to stay. Could you provide beds for a suitable price?"

Mother Antonio skillfully left me in suspense fiddling with the rosary beads hanging from her elaborate habit's waist. Minutes passed. She walked over to the three children who were devouring tamales as if they hadn't had any since they'd left their homes. And probably hadn't. She gestured for milk to be served to all three. Finally she returned to answer my request.

"We have rooms for relatives of patients. We are located very far from the nearest hotels. Are you related to Maria?"

THAT was an unnecessary question. This nun must have learned from a wise Jesuit priest how to probe for answers. With my British accent, Happy's Kentucky yo-alls, and Irina's *Kak ve* she was well aware that none of us hailed from Guatemala. There was method beyond what I imagined.

"No. None of us are related to any of the three girls. They are from Guatemala."

"It is a pity you are not. It is obvious that these Guatemalan girls have traveled to the North of Mexico in hopes of crossing the Border to enter the United States. If they do manage to cross the Border they could go before an immigration judge who might rule on the chance to stay should any one of them have an American-based relation to claim her."

"Ah knows thet," Happy suddenly found her adult voice. She'd been crooning baby talk to the girls, the soothing lullaby-type sound working wonders even though they didn't understand English. Happy showed a different facet to Mother Antonia. She was like a mature jockey back in the saddle in time for an important classic race. "We'uns hahdly knows these gals. We ain't got no knowledge of their folks. Ah's come heah to try t'help them thousands o' kids wut be preyed on by Coyotes. Mebbe Ah c'd help one o' these girls by claimin' huh as one o' mine. Ah's got a dau'tuh close in age."

I interrupted before Happy lost focus by going on about our Dorothy. "Darling, you've got a serious job to do. You must not compromise it."

Mother Antonia nodded as if she knew all about Happy's contract, like a psychic with a particularly brainy client. "Señora Harrow, the

Mexican-United States Border is the most crossed-over Border in the world, with almost one million people crossing back and forth every day for work or tourism in Tijuana alone. Even with one million crossing, your attempt to bring across even one of these three girls would fail. The Texas Governor, Rick Perry, called out National Guardsmen to help the numbers of border patrolmen to catch illegals and send them back to their homelands."

Irina scoffed: "National Guard! With no authority to detain, or arrest!"

Happy stilled her. In that newly adopted mature tone, she said: "Irina, Ah's not plannin' enny il-legal bohduh crossin' but usin' mah pass'poht wut has a pic-ture o' mah Dorothy."

Putting an end to the discussion, Mother Antonia went to Maria and tenderly helped her to leave the chair that was now facing an empty platter where earlier there had been ten tamales. There was blood on the chair. Mother Antonia pretended not to notice the stained seat. In Spanish, she said: "Vamanos, m'hija. Hay que buscar el medico."

Left with the two younger nuns and our two little traveling companions, Happy put it to the nuns that they show us to our rooms.

Irina asked for a bath.

One nun stayed in the dining room to scrub off the blood from Maria's seat. The youngest nun complied with Irina's request and showed her where to bathe: in an out-sized tub that stood on clawed feet in a bathroom the size of a kennel.

Irina put down her tired carry-all, unzipped it to draw out a clean pair of slacks and a new T-shirt. We watched as she reached for a ready bar of soap and a towel and closed the bathroom door.

Happy and I took over a sterile bedroom that smelled of bleach. It was furnished sparsely with a double bed neatly made up with embroidered sheets covered by a thin blanket against the mountain-night. No carpet. No wastebasket or desk. One narrow rattan chair. Over the bed hung a very fine silver plated crucifix. Next to the bed was a wash stand with its soap dish, and bowl. Receiving the fading light from a single window hung a century-old oil painting of the Virgin Mary.

The two little girls from the Mexico City terminal had followed us upstairs. Now they hung back, feeling too shy to enter our room.

"Mi nombre es Angela," whispered the eldest from our door. She was frightened to be separated from us.

The youngest spoke up louder: "Y yo me llamo Flor, mi nombre es Flor. No nos dejen solas."

The nun spoke high school English, but translated well enough. "Angela, the eldest. The youngest's name is Flor. She not wish for you to leave her alone. Her, or Angela."

Happy understood. She'd had to leave our brood plenty of times, and had to watch their smiles fade to dejected frown lines. She used her Epsom way of saying good night to our brood: she hugged both of them and trilled: "Sweet dreams."

Where would these two girls sleep? I reckoned they would bed down in a dormitory.

The young nun said: "They will sleep with our novices. Good night. May God keep you." She made the sign of the cross and disappeared.

I found the one light bulb's switch, turned it off, and collapsed on the thin mattress. There could be no lovemaking with Happy tonight. Not in this convent hospital. Happy made too much noise during lovemaking. She never failed to give with yelps that could be heard throughout a building.

Chapter 7

In the morning I had to choose between my new blue suit or the tired jeans and T-shirt. I chose the jeans and T-shirt. There were no important events in the offing!

Both Happy and I took baths. Not together, not in this convent hospital.

We joined forces to find our way downstairs to the ornate dining hall. There was no one there. However two plates, two knives, with a platter of Mexican bread alongside a pot of honey and two mugs filled with tea and a full teapot waited for us. The tea was lukewarm.

"Ah heahs singin' not fur 'way," Happy had taught our brood not to eat with their mouths full, but she broke her own rule this morning. Her Kentucky drawl came through a mouth crammed with corn bread. "Ah thinks them Gate-ma-lan kids been taken to cha-pel. Yo-all thinks Irina went to cha-pel too?"

"Not your brothel friend, Irina. Surely not. More likely she's gone into town to the Russian Consulate."

"No way. Irina has got t'hide from them folks."

"Or so she told you!"

I smelled Irina before I saw her. She came in bringing with her the two smaller girls. The girls smelled of Tamales, she smelled of perspiration and the odor from between her legs.

Her face alight, she sang out. "To chapel you should have come. Most beautiful. Very good singing, very good songs."

The two girls went for the Mexican bread. When Irina leaned over me to get a slice, her odor grew noticeably more potent. I covered my nostrils with the nearest napkin.

Happy must have smelled those odors too, but she rushed to Irina and gave her a hug. "Hi, yo-all. Ah's plannin' t'see thet chapel latuh. Sorry Ah missed the mu-sic. Sounded real pro-fess-ional! Wheah's Maria? Didn't want' go t'the cha-pel?"

Irina's expression darkened like the sky when a storm covers the sun. "Maria! Very sick. Not from rape. Still hurts her hole, but cleaned out she has been. No. When tests made, Doctor Nun found Maria has tuberculosis. Never she will be admitted to the United States. Maria to isolation ward has gone, sent by Mother Antonia."

Happy, silenced, drooped her shoulders like a canary folds its wings having lost the will to sing.

We exchanged glances. How many hours had we been cooped up in that bus with Maria? And what about Angela? And Flor? I rubbed my unshaven chin, speculating if there was a preventive injection we five could have? Could this convent hospital provide it?

Thinking out loud, I mused: "Why would a sick girl make this grueling trip?"

Irina filled in the blanks. "Her family and village raise money for to go to the United States to take treatment. Visa, she could not get. Now, money for Coyote stolen by bus driver."

"What a mess! What an ending for such a long trip! Happy, I wonder how WE can help Maria." I felt my usually-shaven chest rub its bristles against my T-shirt. I hated the bristles grown on my chest between shaves. The possibility that they could injure Happy's delicate breasts always appalled me, and I made a strict habit of shaving my chest every morning. Puberty had brought an over-abundance of hair to most of my body. Only the soles of my feet and palms of my hands had escaped that infringing forest. My wonderful wife had never complained. When I'd tried to apologize for the unshaven parts, she invariably reminded me that our kids and I were her greatest loves, but then came her horses and THEY certainly had pelts.

Happy sighed deeply, thinking how we worried even when our kids had nothing more than a slight sniffle.

I groaned: "Happy! You're great at getting out of a mess. Any ideas of what to do with these children?"

"Not yet. Rick, yo-all go upstairs n' shave. Put on yourn blue suit 'n propah shoes. Go into the town. Make a reccie. Yo-all c'n pass fo' a bus'nessman. Ah needs t'stay heah with Maria, Angela, and Flor. We'uns got some sortin' t'do."

Irina interrupted, "Mr. Harrow, with you I will come to Ciudad Juarez."

Irina grabbed a piece of bread. She looked at it in a strange way. "Communion I have taken at altar. I wish to be of help to Maria. We will visit largest hospital in city to learn if take tuberculosis patients. This is not convenient for you?"

"Very convenient," I nodded, and headed for the upstairs bedrooms. I was familiar with the Russians' use of that expression: "Not convenient." In this case I considered it a damn good plan to evade the Coyotes' notice by being accompanied by a woman other than Happy.

Mother Antonia telephoned for the taxi driver who'd brought us to her convent hospital. The ubiquitous mobile telephone! Flor and Angela had been gifted one by their grandmother. Odilia got most of her fares by phone. And here was Mother Antonia in a lonely bit of desert blessed with a hospital, and even she had a mobile. "Odilia is a good woman. She has brought abandoned illegals to me before. I think she goes to meet the buses as they arrive from Mexico City, and collects children who are left at the terminal by Coyotes when they bring no money for them. She took the name Odilia because she was losing her eye sight and therefore her livelihood but her sight was restored when she prayed to Saint Odilia."

Happy changd the subject. "Ma'am, wut yo-all think will happen to Maria? Cain't yo-all keep huh heah 'n treat thet tu-ber-cu-losis?"

"No, Mrs. Harrow. Sadly we must send Maria away to a hospital that specializes in the treatment of tubercular patients. There, she might have a chance to stay alive. I wish we knew more about her family. She says she's an orphan, brought up by her mother's mother. A group of her relations chipped in together to give her the money to pay a Coyote to smuggle her across the border. But the money wasn't enough. The bus driver who, uh, abused her, he kept her money too."

MOTHER ANTONIA INTERUPTED HERSELF TO REMOVE HER FALSE TEETH, AND PLACE THEM IN HER POCKET. Did her dentures hurt? Had she tolerated them all day, longing for bedtime as the time to take them out? Had our needs interferred with hers? She gave a little sigh, then continued: "As for Angela and Flor, they too were sent on the thousand-mile journey by their grandmother. They are first cousins. Flor's mother was against the trip. But her mother-in-law won out. That lady gave them just enough money for the bus rides, and some food. This grandmother counted on her renegade son, long gone to Chicago, to collect both girls. But he backed out of helping them when he realized that as a very long time illegal he could be arrested and kept from returning to his job in Chicago. He failed to tell his mother and instead used his mobile phone to tell the girls when they were waiting for him at the Ciudad Juarez terminal!'"

"Do thet mean we'uns c'n mebbe adopt them two?"

"My dear Mrs. Harrow, I doubt you will want to. Flor's nasty sores are highly contagious, they are scabies. We do have the right cure for that. I hope we can clear it up in a few days. As for Rosa, her head has an infestation of lice."

"Golly, gee. Ah sho' glad mah Dorothy don't have nothin' lahke thet."

I know Happy, I'd bet she was thinking that maybe adoption wasn't such a good idea, at least not until both girls were unlikely to infect our Dorothy.

A blatant horn broke our silence. Odilia, the female taxi Samaritan had arrived.

The taxi was cleaner today. Odilia had taken the time to give it a wash. She said in Spanish that she spoke broken English. Irina translated Odilia's opening remark: "You must have hypnotized Mother Antonia. It is a rule at that convent to never keep illegals more than one night."

To set her straight, I said via Irina: "I am not an illegal. I have a visa for the United States."

"And those three unwashed children?"

"You know we met two of them in Mexico City. We know little about them. Only that they came on their own from Guatemala."

"You think they lost the money to pay Coyotes?"

"No. What the eldest brought wasn't enough. Four hundred dollars short. The two younger girls brought no money. They were supposed to be met by an uncle at the bus terminal. He never came. He'd been in the U.S.A. for ten years, but was still an illegal and was afraid of being stopped at the border himself. Didn't show up because he was afraid he could lose his cushy life in Chicago, and his $50,000-a-year job."

"Shall we go to a bank? You will lend the eldest four hundred dollars and enough extra to pay up for a Coyote?"

"No. I'm going about this in what I think is the right way." I signaled with fingertips to my mouth that Irina should not translate everything of what I was going to say next. "Please, just tell Odilia to drive us to the center of the town. Before anything else, we need to get mobile phones. I need to call Epsom to check on the horses I train. Happy needs to find out her next move from the boss."

In Spanish, Irina gave the order. "Drop us at a mobile phone shop."

Odilia nodded, and turned to concentrate on the road, which had suddenly filled with crazy careening traffic.

Irina said: "Good it is, use same taxi. Not sensible to pinpoint our address to these animals you are trying to lose."

I laughed. "The Coyotes? I couldn't say they aren't animals, but more correctly they are gangsters exploiting illegals by promising to take them across the U.S. Border."

"For much money."

"Yes. On average around seven thousand dollars. That's a small fortune for kids, and most adults, to pay. Usually, they have relatives in the United States who will cover the loans they almost invariably have to get. Those illegals are the lucky ones: when they have a U.S.-based relative. If they have a willing relative there's a chance an immigration judge will consider the case, once they give themselves up to a State Trooper."

"For my first job with KGB, I was sent to East Berlin. At that time many East Germans scaled The Wall for freedom in the West. Many killed, shot at wall."

"Happy SAID you worked for the KGB. How did a chapel-loving woman get into that?"

"I, as a child, not permitted to go to any chapel. Always, I wondered what was inside that would cause believers to risk Siberia. I lived with aunt who was strong communist. When we passed any of Leningrad's sublime churches, she tell me I would join my mother in Siberia if ever into a church I went."

"Your mother was sent to Siberia?"

"To a work camp. Never did I see her after age of six. When she died, I was not told. Perhaps soon after arrival, perhaps in ten years.

Certainly before interviewed I was by KGB. My aunt wanted me to have a future in the KGB."

"Weren't interviewers suspicious of a daughter of a woman sent to die in Siberia?"

"Nyet. My aunt big in Communist Party. Clever woman, hard. Had plan. She paid for me to have nose operated to make smaller, less hooked. My chin, built up. KGB sent me to sex school, learn much, put to use in East Berlin."

"Will you be going to the Russian Consulate this morning?"

"No! I know not if there IS a consulate here. Last, but absolute last place I go. All consulates and embassies alerted I am on death list. I want to help Happy. I promise help. I know what that Homburg hat man look like. I warn you when I see. You must accept help. Happy not want lose you."

The mid-morning sun brought intense heat. Like veils dropping from Salomé, the night's cooler breezes fell away.

Irina's stink grew worse. Would she stick as close to me as a kangaroo baby in its mother's pouch? I felt tempted to make my first stop in the town at a drugstore to buy a deodorant for her.

And what did Odilia think of Irina? Was it true Odilia spoke no English? Surely, Irina knew from her Soviet days that most taxi drivers speak various languages and report to the local police what they learn from their fares. Why had Irina spoken out as profusely as she sweated?

Odilia left us at a camera shop that had a display of mobile phones in its window.

Yes, the salesman had what I wanted. Yes, I could plug in its charger using the local electricity. No, he didn't have any ready-charged phones for sale. I bought two iPhones, one for both Harrows, and a standard mobile that was ready-charged by PrepaYed for Irina.

Irina repaid me for hers when we'd left the shop. I'd introduced her to the salesman as my wife, and thought it best to put all three phones on my credit card.

Next, we went to a Farmacia, marked by its green cross above a secure doorway. "No recreational drugs for sale here," I was informed by a surly, bald, elderly pharmacist. He took me for a gringo who had crossed the border for marijuana.

"Razors? Shaving soap? Toothbrushes and a toothpaste?" I needed only one tube of toothpaste: I always shared mine with Happy.

That seemed to accentuate our one-ness.

I felt reluctant to ask aloud for deodorant, although I was damned determined to buy one for Irina to give her for the toiletry bag she'd unpacked next to the claw-footed tub.

With a wink that was overly familiar, the salesman directed us to the appropriate aisles.

Irina had a list from Happy that included remedies for Flor's scabies and a specialty comb with shampoo to weed out Angela's infestation of lice. Suddenly, Irina's hand went for my free arm like a shark hitting a surfer. "Keep your head down, you must. Homburg hat buying condoms in next aisle."

I stole a glance at Homburg hat. He was intent on comparing various types of condoms. There was no need for us to hide. His full attention was on prospective purchases. His aisle offered a wide selection, including condoms that tasted of chocolate.

Irina shoved her purchases into my hands. She left our aisle to enter the condoms'. Using a whore's come-on walk, she sidled next to Homburg hat. Taught the trick while she worked for the KGB, Irina pressed her venus mount against Homburg hat's backside, available to her as he leaned into the condoms' shelves.

He whirled around.

Stared. Recognized a professional whore, and sneered.

"*Usted es demasiada vieja,*" he growled, "*No me interesa. Largase. Para mi no hay que las ninas chiquitas, no mas que de once anos.*" He gave Irina a dismissive shove, while he was telling her to get lost because she was too old, he only liked little girls no older than eleven.

Skillfully, Irina played along, backed away but then stopped. Full stop. She pulled out her shiny new mobile and showed it to Homburg hat. Like an experienced fisherman in a trout stream, she gave him plenty of space before she threw him a hook. "You so handsome! Please you take selfie so I have your picture!" Very slowly she drew close enough to hand him her phone.

For two long seconds he hesitated, but eventually – too vain to refuse to take a selfie – he squared his shoulders and cocking the hat higher on his forehead he showed off his know-how of selfies to take his own photograph.

Wriggling her behind in the style she had often used to escape an unsavory John in Mississippi Madam's brothel, Irina faked an effort to kiss him in thanks. He pulled away only far enough to be able to still hand back the mobile. She made a little girl's curtsey, blew him a safe kiss, and carefully headed for the neon-lit cosmetics counter.

She lurked there, permitting him to juggle his preference in condoms, walk leisurely to the pharmacist, and pay.

He never looked to where I spied at him from between two bottles of Listerine.

When he left the Farmacia, Irina winged to my side crowing with a victorious chirp. "DNA, fingerprints, all on mobile case! Picture good, I checked."

Irina demanded we wait a fraught ten minutes before I paid for my razors, shaving cream, toothpaste and the deodorant.

We had a bad surprise outside the Farmacia. Homburg hat was still in viewing distance. We belted for a grove of Poinciana trees, hoping their masses of red blossoms would screen us. Homburg hat had collected his Maserati from the upper level of a two-storey parking lot but was held captive by an argumentative cashier who'd refused to raise the exit barrier before this customer paid up.

We could hear their raucous voices, that sounded like two macaws squawking. Homburg hat kept insisting he was being over charged.

While Irina waited to be able to photograph Homburg hat's Maserati, and its license plate, I asked: "Irina, how could he need so many condoms?"

It wasn't a very tactful question to put to this recent inmate of a brothel, but I couldn't resist.

"*Da*, good question. *Oche harasho*. But not funny. You recall chicken pox outbreak that shut down a rehab facility for illegals in New Mexico most recently? Much talk on news about it. Homburg hat must be worried he could catch venereal disease from raping the children he promises to take across the border."

"Only, promises?"

"*Da*. This Homburg hat, he look coward. Not type to swim the Rio Grande. Quick. Hold purchases while I take picture." The Maserati was still stuck at the parking lot's pay-out cabin while Homburg hat argued over the parking fee. Now he threw down a handful of pesos, the barrier rose, and Irina caught the car and its license plate on her mobile's camera.

"We go to police. We have evidence, they get pictures, DNA, and fingerprints."

I checked on the pictures. They were as good as if taken by a Leica. They permitted me to study Homburg's face. It was ugly, although he believed Irina when she declared it handsome. He had been in many fights. His nose was broken. There were trenches above his sliced eyebrows. His lips had bulges from scar tissue. "What evidence? Evidence of what?"

"He be Coyote. We have Angela and Flor at convent hospital. They give evidence."

Reluctant to include our two little friends from the Mexico City terminal to be used as witnesses of how Homburg hat had collected other illegal children from their bus, nevertheless I acted on Irina's cue.

She loaned her mobile, but refused to enter the impressive police station to which we were promptly directed. Armed with the temporary papers provided by my embassy in Mexico City, I walked in to that lions' den as purposefully as if I'd just saddled a prize colt to accompany him down to Ascot's pre-race paddock.

Irina scuttled across the street to look for ladies' underwear shops. Happy had ordered two bras and three pairs of panties.

The uniformed minion at the police desk was surly. I'll bet he spoke English, but he held to his idea of high ground by diminishing my stature choosing Spanish only. The British Embassy's official DIEU ET MON DROIT escutcheon on my papers had failed to sway him.

"*Que quiere? Esto no es un hotel para turistas.*"

"I am not a tourist. I am here to nail a Coyote. Please direct me to your superior officer." No one appeared in order to help by translating.

Didn't matter. The minion's arrogant expression, lips curled like a crocodile's, told the story. Apparently, I wasn't to get help promptly.

Minutes passed before a lazily postured Mexican dragged his legs from an inner room. He snarled at me: "No time for ridiculous claims. Go back to your British Isles. The only Brits we want to see here are William and Kate."

It took a couple of seconds for me to realize he referred to Their Royal Highnesses the Duke and Duchess of Cambridge. I shouldn't have felt so astonished. Looking past the surly minion, I saw a Herald Post clipping featuring William and Kate, with their baby George, tacked to the grimy wall. What? Even here in Ciudad Juarez, over-run by illegal immigrants and Coyotes, this royal couple's newspaper photo adorned a wall?

This police captain was a *nasty*. Like many an Englishman I took note of his clothes: they weren't off the rack, they were made to measure by an expert tailor. Same style as the minion's, but with a highly expensive difference. His hair was worn just grazing his collar, almost like a client of TRUMPER'S of London. He hadn't bothered to shave, a hefty beard was lurking to come through. His eyes, probing and worldly-wise, showed no soul. His mouth was greedy, there were slivers of spit in the corners. He was a five foot five person, but gave the impression he stood three inches taller. Maybe he favored elevator shoes.

Where had he mined for his apparent wealth?

The answer came as I stood up from my seat to shake hands. While noting his fingers weren't washed, I simultaneously gave my attention to the arrival of two six-feet-tall policemen who had entered cursing, dragging a little girl. Judging by my own Dorothy's age, I judged this child to be between nine and ten. Her clothes had been brutally ripped, but had originally been of top quality. Not made in the U.S.A., but more likely in a Central American country, because her ripped totally torn dress had a considerable amount of hand embroidery. She had one shoe, the other foot gave away a horror story: it was a very bloodied sock. Looking closer, I saw that raw red blood was oozing down to the sock.

"*Llevala donde siempre,*" the captain barked. His policemen, from apparent experience, continued to drag the child while the desk minion helped them by shoving her two shoulders. The entire scene had erupted over less than a minute.

No newcomer to this, the captain made a show of passing it off as an everyday occurrence: which, with dread, I thought it could be. This little girl would be worth money. The family, who had sent her to the U.S. border, would pay plenty to get her back – raped, or not.

To break a meaningful silence, I said: "I have come here with important information. By chance a guest of mine was able to get pictures of a Jackal. And his car, showing its license number. We also may have his fingerprints on a phone. We first saw him when we arrived by bus from Mexico City: he had come to herd illegal children on the next part of the journey meant to take them across the border." With a florid meaningful gesture, I drew Irina's mobile from my jacket's handkerchief pocket. "I have here a photograph of a Coyote who collected thirteen illegal children from a bus based in Mexico City. His fingerprints and DNA are on this mobile's case. Please have them processed before they get lost."

"Video of this Coyote *with* children coming out of a bus marked Ciudad Mexico?"

"No. The picture is a still, and there are no children in it. But I know where there are three girls between the ages of seven and eleven who also came on that bus and they were witnesses. One of the three, the eleven-year-old, was raped by the driver of that bus during our last rest stop before arriving in Ciudad Juarez. I was on that bus, and I am a witness to the girl being taken by the driver to a shed and later returning with her skirt bloodied. I am prepared to swear to that before a judge."

The minion's eyes came alight, revealing indisputably that he understood English. He brought out a notepad and a chewed pencil that had its lead intact. Clearly interested by the latter part of the story, the rape, he asked: "Do you have photograph of bus driver?"

"No. But this witness, Maria, the eleven-year-old rape victim, told me he was taking his bus to a nearby town called Nuevas Casas Grandes for an overhaul and to disinfect its interior." I didn't want to pinpoint Maria as a seriously contagious passenger, but I felt I had to give some idea of the scope of the need for hygienic cleaning. "There were children on the bus with highly contagious problems: scabies, lice, and a very serious case of tuberculosis. One had red spots, could have been the onset of chicken pox."

Tuberculosis, scabies, lice and possibly chicken pox were of no interest. He wanted to hear more about the rape. His eyes glistened disgustingly when I returned to that horror.

"The eleven-year-old wasn't admitted to this Coyote's minivan. She HAD brought money for him. It wasn't enough. She was short six thousand six hundred dollars."

"You do know where she is now?" He asked this as if he was ready to jump on his motorcycle and rape her again.

"I'm not sure. My wife and I had flagged down a taxi, and drove with her to a hospital to have her wounds dealt with. She was bleeding still, and heavily. Very torn, or so she tried to tell my wife. She wouldn't speak to me. She sat as far away from me as she could, terrified of any man."

"*Carambas*! *Hijo de puta*! That was yesterday. Not twenty-four hours ago," the arrogant officer intervened in a tobacco-hoarse voice. "Tell me the name of the hospital. She must still be there."

Using her illness as an excuse, I disagreed: "This pathetic child needed additional medical help not available in the hospital we took her to. I never saw her after she left the taxi and was wheeled away on a gurney." That last was not true. I'd been in the dining hall with Maria, and seen the bloody stain she'd left on her chair.

"What was the additional medical help that she needs. Come into my office and I will run off on my computer all the names of hospitals in our State of Chihuahua."

"I'm sorry. I can't help you further. I'll wait outside while you take the driver's DNA and fingerprints from my friend's mobile. Then I am going to meet that friend for lunch. Locally. If you need me, my name is Harrow. I'll be staying at the Hotel Plaza." I spoke as firmly as if I'd been warning one of my racehorse owners that he must geld his favorite colt. I used my "give no quarter" tone of voice and stepped outside to stand on the crumbling sidewalk until Irina's mobile was returned to me. I had given the police the name of Ciudad Juarez's finest watering place. Long ago I'd learned that the best address is the one to use when dealing with nasties.

No thanks given. None expected.

After it was returned, I tucked Irina's mobile into my pocket and crossed the street to winkle Irina out of the lingerie shop. I could believe that lingerie is a big deal for a former brothel inmate. Irina, laden with packages in bags with logos, looked delighted when I told her we would be moving to the Hotel Plaza.

First, I had to endure a lengthy process to acquire a rental car. After an hour of arranging for local insurance and giving enough personal data to entice hackers, we loaded it up with the purchases, which had their logo-bright bags ripped open by the Hotel Plaza's reception clerk to ascertain they held no drugs. My papers, acquired three days ago at the British Embassy, had no photos on them which meant I passed off Irina as my wife without incident.

I always get a thrill from visiting a new city. When I'm accompanied by Happy my sex life improved in a new bed, *if* it isn't located in a convent hospital. On this trip I got some pleasure from seeing the Franklin star up above El Paso's skyline.

There was no hanky panky with Irina. We ate our Mexican too-fresh beef in near silence, Irina not wishing to give away her Russian background by her accent.

We stared at a fine view of Mount Franklin framed by our restaurant's picture window. On our table was a cardboard take-home detailing El Paso's and Ciudad Juarez's histories. I learned that Alvaro Nuñez Cabeza de Vaca marched into this prime spot on the Rio Grande in 1536, having been disappointed in his attempt to explore what is now Florida. Two hundred and fifty years of Spanish rule followed. Eventually the French came, with their figurehead Emperor Maximilian, who would be killed by one of Mexico's first revolutions. I skipped the details about the first successful ranches and oil gushers, more intrigued by the account of its Prohibition Era and how bootleggers refined the schemes of this area's long reigning smugglers. Were today's Coyotes in the mold of those earlier gangsters?

Irina insisted on paying for her lunch. "I am tired of hoarding money. Let us go now to shop for girls' dresses to buy miniskirt style that American wear. Flor and Angela must not keep to their Guatemalan calf-length skirts."

"I agree. Two complete outfits for each."

"And, Maria?"

"I doubt she'll get out of hospital gowns for some time. We'll buy an iPad suitable for an eleven-year-old."

The restaurant's cashier pointed out a department store.

We spent too much time choosing the girls' clothes.

The iPad was easy. We went back to the camera shop where I'd bought my iPhones.

Interesting Irina in Ciudad Juarez was no snap. I'd retrieved my rental car from the hotel parking lot. The city's downtown was marked by screeching tires, crazy drivers, swearing policemen and zombie-like pedestrians obsessed by their mobiles. Escaping the worst traffic, a pleasant tranquility washed over us as we cruised past the graceful Spanish-Colonial mission Church of Our Lady of Guadalupe. Built in 1650 by the founder of the mission, Fray Garcia, its sublime architecture touched a need in Irina.

"Stop! You will stop, please. I wish to enter that church."

Irina got her wish. I couldn't hope to park anywhere nearby, and it proved difficult to circle back. Swerving to avoid hitting a peon on a donkey loaded with firewood, I looked down a side street – and Great God -- there was Hombug hat's Maserati, idling in front of a liquor store.

Homburg hat was NOT in jail.

He emerged from the liquor store to take the wheel of the very noticeable car.

I collected a subdued Irina from in front of the mission church's glorious façade. Driving in the opposite direction of the Maserati, I followed the example of what every other driver was doing: I broke the speed laws.

When we reached the convent hospital, I borrowed the method used by the Mississippi Madam's Johns to hide a car. I chose the laundry area where dozens of sheets flapped in the afternoon breeze. Irina and I entered the convent to the sound of nuns' hands slapping old-fashioned wash boards. I smelled bleach and detergent.

At an ironing board, dealing with a pile of pillowcases, the young nun from yesterday gave a welcome back twinkle. I crossed to her and handed over the extra iPad. "For Maria," I said. "I know I am not allowed in the Isolation Area. I'd like her to know she isn't forgotten."

Happy heard my voice, found me and hurried me out of the laundry area: that white refuge from dirt and disease.

Angela and Flor met us in the main hall. Happy had turned them into replicas of our daughter, Dorothy. She had cut off their braids, created curls falling to their shoulders and they each had a half-fringe partly covering their foreheads.

"Rick-Honey, Ah's been turrible worried fo' yo-all. Yo-all's been gone hours 'n hours. Get anythin' done?" She hugged me with the intensity of a winter flower reaching for the sun.

"Yes, and no. I got you an iPhone so you can call the kids. You'll have to charge it, first. I went to a chemist's for tooth brushes and toothpaste and almost bumped into Homburg hat. He was buying condoms in a nearby aisle. Irina flirted with him, got his picture on her new mobile. DNA, fingerprints: the lot! We took her mobile to the police. I thought Homburg hat'd be nabbed within minutes. Well, if the Mexican police even detained him at all, it wasn't for long. Irina and I just saw him in his Maserati in downtown Ciudad Juarez."

Irina showed her the picture she'd taken of Homburg hat. Happy had a long look.

Another facet of Happy's character over-rode her fascination with the photo. She'd noticed the packages Irina carried. Two of the packages, in blaring pink cardboard boxes, had the name of a famous designer who specialized in children's wear. "Kids stuff?" she asked, hopefully, her generous heart working overtime like a busy harvester. "Yo-all noticed how Ah's changed them kids' hair-do. Now fo' a purty dress fo' each gal."

"*Da*. Pink packages have kids' skirts and shirts. Bras and panties in anonymous brown bags for you." Irina gave one pink package to Angela. The smaller pink package went to Flor.

Irina didn't open the packages. She knew from her own poverty scarred childhood how much it meant to a girl to open a present that was going to be her very own.

Mother Antonia silently joined our group. When two miniscule miniskirts emerged like butterflies from their chrysalis of tissue paper, both girls turned with mixed expressions to search for Mother Antonia's approval.

No frown. Instead, a gentle smile. "If those skirts get you girls across the border, I am pleased that Irina bought them."

A good sport, Mother Antonia!

I said: "Good afternoon, Mother. Thank you again for looking after my wife and these girls. We'd like to stay longer with you, but I understood from your favorite taxi driver that you limit stays to one day and one night. I believe we'll be overstaying our welcome. As for Maria, I hope you'll keep her here after you feel she's had the treatment she needs. I've thought of a Foundation that underwrites the costs of a sick child who needs a lengthy treatment. I'll contact the Foundation for you on Maria's behalf. I'll be writing to you."

Mother Antonia nodded but her wrinkles gave a negative dance. Sorry to see us leave? Despairing of any Foundation's help for Maria?

A bell announced vespers. Irina blocked Mother Antonia's departure. "Blessing, please. Give me your blessing."

Irina knelt on the hall's cool antique tiles. Mother Antonia made the sign of the cross above her head, then left.

With a quizzical grin, Irina followed us upstairs to pack. She muttered: "Blessing backward. Blessing left to right, should be right to left."

◇ ◇ ◇

None of us had much to pack.

Happy had reacted to the panties in much the same way as the girls had to their miniskirts. "Ah cain't say Ah will wear these things." She held them up for me to study. They had a circle of string intersecting with another string that had a stamp-sized piece of cloth. The cloth looked like the half inch of gauze inside a band-aid. "Ah don't know wut a whore's panties look lahke, but Ah's feared thet's wut she done bought fo' me."

"One favor," I said. "We bought a special comb to rake out lice. Could you give Angela's new hairdo a little help with the comb?"

"Ain't much t'ask. Both girls need baths. Angela c'n have a shampoo 'n then Ah'll git me busy with that there comb."

When we arrived at the Hotel Plaza, all five of us looked presentable. Irina had masked her smell with perfume. I'd given my chin and cheeks a proper shave. Happy was in her Mexico City blouse tucked into the miniskirt Angela had passed on.

Angela and Flor wore convent school uniforms found by Mother Antonia in a suitcase left over from her days as the headmistress of an El Paso school. That clever lady had explained: "The border guards will not be expecting illegals to appear in the famous uniform of a prestigious El Paso school."

We had dinner upstairs, brought by the Hotel Plaza's room service. Not a good idea to show ourselves in the main dining room or the coffee shop! Risky. And I had two little girls to protect, in addition to a much-beloved wife.

Strange, but later as I was falling asleep, all I could think of was that Happy showed good sense in accepting Angela's miniskirt. Angela was well rid of it. She hadn't forgotten that Maria had been raped with less provocation than for wearing a miniskirt. Like Popocatepetl, a rapist could become active at any time.

Chapter 8

By dawn my iPhone had been fed with enough juice for me to ring Epsom for news from my Head Lad.

Nothing out of the ordinary had happened at stables in the past three days.

"Sir, Mr. Harrow Sir, the two-year-olds are coughing. ANCHOR II has a chilblain. Oh, but Sir I'd like a word with Mrs. Harrow. There's been several calls for her from the same racing agent. I believe she is being offered a ride in Ascot's White Rose stakes. The owner wants her on this side of the pond to familiarize herself with his horse."

"Mrs. Harrow isn't here, Tom. She's gone for a swim. I'll pass on the message. I know which agent you mean."

I'd replaced the receiver precisely when Happy returned.

She looked anxious. "Wut yo-all talkin' to Tom concernin' me? An agent? Which agent? Aw, yo-all c'n tell me latuh. Rick-Honey, theah's somethin' urgent: Ah's seen a rash on me. Ah thinks as mebbe Ah done caught them scabies from Flor." She removed the borrowed towel robe, and pointed to her stomach. Her skimpy bikini revealed a double stripe of red bumps like miniature railroad tracks. They marched across her stomach, ruining that sublime white flesh exactly where I most loved to kiss it. "Does yo-all think as we'uns should go back to Mother Antonia's hospital?."

"No. There's a doctor's office across the street. We'll try that first. But let me cheer you up: Tom wanted a word because the agent – who is old Blumfield – he's got you a ride for Ascot's White Rose Stakes." I didn't add that the owner of this special colt wanted Happy in England, now, to familiarize herself with the colt.

Happy's renowned good spirits faded further. She bit her lip. "Ah cain't ride if'n Ah's got them scabies."

"Don't worry, darling. If you can bear the scabies, I'm sure the colt won't object to you having the ride. It's ringworm that I dread, where any of my string is concerned. Come on, put on some clothes and we'll go give this Ciudad Juarez doctor a try. But leave Flor with Irina. The doctor might be leary of catching scabies."

We were admitted promptly to the doctor's inner sanctum. Elderly, belonging very much to an earlier era, he wore pince-nez spectacles attached to a black ribbon hooked to the back of one ear. He never smiled. He barely spoke. He appeared to be overly-modest when it came time for Happy to remove her panties. Without touching her stomach, either from over-zealous modesty or for fear of scabies, he made a quick job of examining the double tracks of red pimples. Replacing the old fashioned magnifying glass used for that purpose, after a very cursory examination, he removed his spectacles, blew on them, and polished the lenses with a huge handkerchief: "Señora," he said with careful Nineteenth Century courtesy, "I need to know what you ate for dinner yesterday evening."

"Tortilla filled with shrimp, Sir."

"Ah, well then, I believe you have an allergy to shrimp. My respects, Señora. You may pay the bill as you go out."

I looked at my watch.

"Ten to ten. Two hours before checking out time!" I whispered in Happy's perfectly unblemished ear: "We have time to make love. Come, on. Let's go back to our room before twelve."

I guessed right that Happy would now enjoy a double high: being offered a ride at Ascot in the White Rose Stakes, and being free of scabies.

We made beautiful love. I ALWAYS enjoy a new bed in a strange city's hotel, but it's even better when Happy's on a high.

Interrupting a delicious afterglow, Happy left our bed to unpack her iPhone. She punched in Hannibal's number, one that she'd meticulously typed in to her list of Recents. He'd been the second call she'd made on that iPhone. The first would always be to our kids.

It was also her second call to him in the morning. She'd had to leave a message when there'd been no reply earlier. This time I could hear his grating voice and her polite responses. When the call ended, Happy did not return to my arms. She headed for another shower. Stopping in the bathroom's doorway, she said slowly: "Cur'ous. He wants us to go raght away t'Columbus, New Mex'co. Rick-Honey, yo-all knows wheah-all this New Mex'co be?"

"Sure. Next state west of Texas. I'll get you there. But we'll have to send Irina and the two girls via Mexico by bus to Puerto Palomas, the border town to New Mexico, across the way from Columbus."

"Another long bus rahde? Po' little girls. Po' Irina."

"Maybe we shouldn't try to keep Angela and Flor. The Mexican authorities should send them back to Guatemala. That's not our job. You need to follow up on the Coyotes. Irina? We can't really involve ourselves in *her* life."

"Darlin', as Ah re-calls: she already done in-volved husself in ourn."

Happy almost always gets the last word. This time it was simple for Happy to get her way.

She disappeared into the bathroom.

Chapter 9

By twelve noon I'd checked out of the Hotel Plaza and was driving Happy back to the convent hospital before we headed toward New Mexico. Happy wanted to see how Maria had weathered the night.

She came armed with three bus tickets to Puerto Palomas for Irina, Flor and Angela to use once they'd given thanks and a tearful goodbye to Mother Antonia.

I paid the convent hospital's very fair bill. After giving out boxes of cookies for distribution to all the nuns, Irina and the two girls were packed into the rental car.

I drove them to yet another bus terminal. I settled them into the right bus, while Happy told them they were heading for Puerto Palomas.

"Yo-all should enjoy goin' theah," She swiveled as if she was on a piano stool to shout to them over the horrendous lunch hour traffic. In Ciudad Juarez its citizens still took off to go to their homes to eat a prolonged lunch or make love during the siesta. "Ah's googled New Mex'co on mah iPhone. It be a real interestin' place. It were in Roswell, New Mex'co that the only ver-i-fiable aliens landed on planet earth."

That caught Irina's attention. She'd looked extremely downcast at the news of leaving for an even smaller town. Basically a Big City woman, Irina scorned small towns in much the same way she'd hate being stuck with a pekinese if there was a gigantic wolfhound available. She brightened now: "Aliens!"

Irina translated "Aliens" for the girls' benefit.

Angela, who had completed Third Grade, where space ships and aliens had been discussed, chirped: "Aliens, which aliens?"

Happy placed an arm around both girls, drawing them to her like a magnet pulls metal splinters. Flor had begun to weep. SHE wasn't eager to hear about aliens. She was rocking from her hips to her heels, repeating over and over: "*Quiero ir a mi Mama, quiero ir a mi Mama.*"

Our Dorothy had often repeated that same plaintive plea in English. "I want to go to Mummy." Knowing there could be a long wait for the bus to leave, Happy used a ploy that had worked with Dorothy, she kept on the same subject to divert Flor.

Happy's motherly heart was torn like a sheet caught by a nail: "Yup, aliens. Them wut crashed in the spaceship they'uns landed in, just outside Roswell, New Mex'co. Happened after the Nevada desert were used to test how a atom bomb would ex-plode. There be folks wut believes them aliens wuz int-er-ested in thet atom bomb 'xpolsion, got lost ovuh New Mex'co 'n crashed.'

Now Irina's attention was as truly caught as a dolphin in a fisherman's net. "I never heard of connection to atom bomb tests! Not told to us in Russia. *Da*, I HAVE heard of aliens. What did these look like?"

"Size o' dwarf. Greenish skin. But they wuz daid when found. Mebbe them had bettuh color skin when they's alive. The size we'uns knows fo' sho. Folks in Roswell asked th'carpentuh wut su-pplied their caskets. Too sho't fo' adult caskets. Needed chillun-size caskets."

Their bus driver tooted his vehicle's horn announcing imminent departure. Happy half-lifted Flor from her seat in an overly frantic hug. There was no way this child was going to stop crying. Happy gave Flor one last kiss, and Irina sat down to play mother. When the bus pulled out of the terminal it was only Angela who waved from a window.

My iPhone supplied navigation help. We returned to Ciudad Juarez to make a less-than-noteworthy border crossing. At the Leaving Mexico, Entering U.S.A. signs, the uniformed agent waved us into the United States after no more than the most minimal glance at my British papers.

Traffic thinned out considerably as we left the El Paso limits to look for the Florida Mountains that would mark the proximity to the town selected by Hannibal: Columbus, population under two thousand, its only fame that it was raided by the Mexican revolutionary Pancho Villa.

Arriving at the outskirts, I saw an odd hovel. It was topped by a separate roof, held in place by poles. It had a sign lettered PANCHO

VILLA HISTORIC SITE. It was our welcome to the State of New Mexico.

We found the hotel Happy had booked via the internet: BERTHA'S. That also had a sign: HOMESTYLE Food.

Happy checked in, while I parked the rental car. When I joined Happy at the reception desk, the reception clerk asked suspiciously: "No suitcases?"

I wondered whether he thought we were illegals, or if we'd come to spend a dirty weekend.

Happy hurried me to our room, "We'uns got no tahme fo' vittels. Them little girls maght be arrivin' in thet Puerto Palomas place. Turrible they couldn'a go theah in ourn car with us'n. But thet Hannibal, he insisted we cross the border 'n drive on the U.S.A. side. Which Irina 'n the kids couldn't do. We-all should hurry up 'n make the bohduh crossin' to Mexico."

"No darling. Their bus isn't non-stop. It will be in Puerto Palomas a good hour later than we arrived here. Puerto Palomas is only about twenty miles away. How about we spend the extra time by having a nice cuddle?"

"Nah. Not with only half an hour to spare! 'N yo-all be the one alw's remahndin' me to keep fo-cused on mah Coyotes job."

Happy didn't bother to unpack the new bras and panties. She probably didn't want the hotel chambermaid to see them, because she still thought the thong panties were styled for a whore. But did this hotel even have a chambermaid on duty?

We used our spare half hour to take showers. Happy had been right: there would have been no time for truly great lovemaking. Any extra minutes were used to fill the car's tank with petrol, and clean its windshield of an appalling layer of desert dust.

A glow from its lights distinguished Puerto Palomas before we reached it. After driving for miles across bleak, stygian desert it cheered us to see Puerto Palomas's old-fashioned neon signs and a boulevard with its fanciful center studded with high past-their-prime lampposts.

My iPhone's navigator told me to take a right at a corner with a huge sign marked DENTISTA. We found Irina, Angela and a weeping Flor standing outside the bus terminal like kindergarten children bereft of a teacher, lost during an outing.

Irina's smile broke out like the sun rising from a bleak horizon. "Thank God you've come!"

I parked the rental car I'd got in Columbus, pulling up level with the girls. Irina helped Happy load in Flor and Angela: two sleepy girls as tired as if they'd been on a picnic.

Flor had stopped crying when she recognized Happy, but now her head drooped with the approach of sleep.

"Our'n ho-tel in Col-umbus rec'mended the PANCHO VILLA heah. Lets us'n see if theah be room fo' yo-all."

Again the navigator did its stuff. I off-loaded the girls, and Irina. Happy stayed with me while I found the Hotel PANCHO VILLA parking lot.

There was one double bedroom available. "Yes, we can put a cot in it for the littlest girl," an English-speaking receptionist told me. I paid in advance for one night, because she'd also raised eyebrows at the fact there was no luggage. I reckoned the woman, mature and kindly, had guessed immediately that the two girls were illegals. Their El Paso convent school uniforms, provided by Mother Antonia, hadn't fooled her. She'd seen all kinds of disguises used by the illegals of all ages who came to Puerto Palomas as a likely place to cross the border.

The room was adequate. Irina frowned at the fact she would have to share the double bed with Angela. I imagine she'd had her surfeit of double beds. No cause for worrying about Angela's lice: she was no longer in the catching phase. Live lice had been slaughtered leaving only their eggs.

I waited with Happy for Flor's cot to arrive, for it to be made up with sheets, and for Happy to tuck Flor between them.

Angela wouldn't undress in front of me. Nodding at Happy and Irina, I said: "I'll meet you two in the bar. I'm sure there must be one."

Happy left a night light on for Angela. Irina lent her the PrePaYed mobile we'd bought in Ciudad Juarez. "You call, I come," Happy told Angela.

The bar was within yards of their double room. In its darkened atmosphere of black leather stools and black enamel-painted tables smelling of ashtrays filled with cheap Mexican cigarettes, I hoped our welcome party would be brief.

"You have spoken to your Mr. Hannibal?" Irina started the conversation, once the waiter had taken our drinks orders.

"Hann'bal? Sho have. Soon's the iPhone were juiced up. He say 'leave Te-xas.' We's to go t'border town in New Mex'co. Name of Columbus. But, yo-all git a creepy feelin' a-bout this? Why he call me? He lost faith in mah pro-fesional-ism?"

Professionalism is a big word for my Happy. Was *she* having second thoughts about working for Hannibal? God only knows. Happy, a big talker to our children, particularly at meal times when they're either screaming for more or refusing to eat, usually keeps her sleuthing to herself.

I smiled. "I don't mind if he telephones, unless it's when we're in the middle of making love."

Irina ignored my remark. She shook her head. "I not like change orders. Why he not like us stay in Ciudad Juarez where close to Coyote you call Homburg hat?"

"Don't make no sense. But ohduhs be ohduhs."

Happy had drawn breath to speak out more on the subject of Hannibal, but whatever she was about to say was obliterated by a white-haired small fat American woman, who -- *un*invited -- drew up a chair to our table. "Hi," the woman gulped, "I'm here in Mexico on my own. You don't mind if I join you!"

We did mind, but the little woman seemed so eager to talk that not one of us had the heart to shut her up and tell her to go away. She was wearing a printed polyester dress that hung three inches below her knees, 1980s' style. Her fingernails were bitten to the edges. Her white hair had grown way past its cutting time.

"Yo-all want a drink? Usn's ordered tequila, wut's 'xpected heah in Mex'co."

The woman nodded, pleased. Then she opened her mouth wide and tapped a rear tooth. "Beautiful work, wouldn't you say? Just the right color. Not too white, or, like an old piano key, yellow. I come here from El Paso for all my dental needs. Cheaper here, and the workmanship is good too."

Irina tried to ignore her but the small woman had a big appetite for company. Between rapid sips of her tequila drink, she introduced herself. "My name's Myra. I'd like to know the names of all three of you. Is the gentleman married," she paused to fill her hand with peanuts from the center of the table, "to either of you ladies?"

With Happy nodding and showing off her wedding ring, Myra kept on like a sailboat in a regatta. "I buy my cigarettes here, Marlboros. No tax on them, of course. When I was a girl during World War II, my folks used to come to Puerto Palomas to get meat and leather shoes. They were scarce items by 1945."

Happy, who like a puppy liked everybody unless they proved to be evil, made the mistake of encouraging Myra. "Wuz yourn folks in Columbus when thet Pancho Villa raided it?"

"No, but my grandparents knew him. He was welcome in their little parcel – you couldn't call it a real ranch. He would come inside and eat their *frijoles* with them." She swallowed a mouthful of chewed peanuts, her interest now swerving to study Irina. Her eyes grew sharp. They were working away like knitting needles trying to finish a sweater without dropping a stitch. In a new, malicious tone, she asked: "And how did you two ladies meet? One of you with a Kentucky hillbilly accent, the other sounding something European. Where and how did you meet?"

Consternation! Happy looked down at the floor. She was never shy about reining in a horse, but the thought of mentioning Mississippi Madam's brothel fazed her. It was Irina who took the bit between clenched jaws like the favorite in a horserace determined to win. No doubt, Irina had been queried as to her background on many another evening.

Figuratively skating on thin ice, Irina spat out: "In Mexico City. A neighbor was driving Mrs. Harrow home from a dinner at the British Embassy, when an unexpected danger to her arose. Mrs. Harrow came next door to us."

Myra asked: "Us? And who was us? You lived with your husband next door?"

Enough. I put a stop to this embarrassing interrogation. I paid the bill and stood up, bowing to Myra. She didn't rate the neck creased head down that I reserve for my monarch. This bow was tendered as a goodbye.

We saw Irina to the bedroom she shared with the girls. Happy peered inside to be assured they were soundly asleep, gave Irina a thumbs up. She didn't even whisper a Good Night to Irina, cautious not to wake either girl.

I walked into the night to go to where the rental car was parked. I thought we'd seen the last of Myra. No, she was standing like petrified wood blocking the front door. She opened her mouth, pointed to a gaping hole, and shoved out the palm of her hand. Her back tooth's new crown nestled there like a pearl in an oyster. "I cracked my new cap finishing the peanuts." The so perfect white piece of porcelain was not attractive now. It was in the wrong place, ugly in her hand whereas before it had served a shining purpose in her mouth.

Myra, having difficulty speaking without a temporary replacement *in situ*, was whining to anyone who would listen in the crowded lobby: "Son of a gun, lousy dentist, used cheap glue for my cap!"

Happy, being Happy, gave her a hug in sympathy before joining me. I was looking forward to making the return trip to Columbus in record time. I burned to be in bed with Happy, in that unfamiliar town.

Chapter 10

When lovemaking is on the agenda, I don't let lonely strangers interfere. I made short work of Myra and her dental crisis, swept Happy into the rental car and sped back to our Columbus hotel.

I kissed Happy into bed, and blasted away with the force of an Apollo spacecraft heading for the moon. Bliss!

Our afterglow didn't last. We'd had a long, blissful afterglow following our initial lovemaking, but Happy's iPhone burped. At two a.m. in the morning! Who the hell had the temerity to call MY wife at two a.m.?

Hannibal.

I didn't speak to him. Happy did, it was her iPhone that rang. We didn't share our iPhones any more than some couples share their toothbrushes.

Falling asleep, partly due to my delicious exertions of the last few hours and partly due to the endless-seeming drive to and from Puerto Palomas, I barely listened to Happy's comments. I couldn't hear Hannibal's.

"Yes, Suh. No, no Suh. Abs'lutely not, Suh. Have a good trip, Suh." No explanation. Nothing except Happy's soft, sweet back finally pressed against mine with a gentle rocking like a canoe in a sun-washed lake. I fell asleep.

Over breakfast, Happy was still not forthcoming. Room service had supplied waffles and maple syrup. Happy crunched away with spaniels' eyes. Maple syrup? When we were so far from Vermont?

She never looked at her iPhone. Never gave a hint of what was said at two bloody a.m.

A flashing red light at the base of our intercom caught my attention. I asked the hotel operator to put me through. The call was from Irina.

"Rick, *kak ve*? When are you coming back to see us?"

Happy had placed her maple--syrup-sticky mouth on my bare shoulder to listen, jostling me from the receiver. Now she shook her head. Negative. She sent me an enigmatic glance. I knew that glance. It meant "No, we aren't going to Puerto Palomas." The enigma was, why not?

She took the phone and asked: "How're them li'l girls? Sleep all through?"

"Slept until daylight. Market day, here. I think should go get new dresses, shoes, underpants for girls. I need new things too."

"Naw. Not if yo-all gits across the bohduh somehow. Ah's goin' shoppin' heah. Impo'tant thet dresses fo' yo-all be made in the good ole U.S.A. Shoes, too. Give yourn act away, Mexican shoes. Ah'll buy sandals, don't mattuh so much t'git them sizes raght. Yeah, sandals."

I noticed that Happy didn't mention underpants. I was damned sure HAPPY wouldn't buy 'whore's panties' for the little girls. If Irina did, Happy would throw them in the nearest bin.

"Ah's stuck heah in C'lumbus. Ohduhs. But Rick c'n hit the road in a hour. Cain't yo-all, Rick Honey?"

I nodded. What else could I do? For one thing, when Happy made up her mind to go shopping, there would be no stopping her: like a maiden two-year-old filly who'd race to her stall for oats.

She continued: "Theah be somethin' else. Irina, Ah needs the tel'phone numbuh o' thet uncle o' the little girls wut lives in Chicago." After she scribbled the number on a pad, Happy said goodbye tenderly, as if Irina was wanting in the affection department. She dressed in her jeans and T-shirt, and dialed the uncle's Chicago number on her iPhone. She didn't use the hotel's switchboard.

When she heard a gruff male Latino voice yelling "Hola," she gave the uncle Hell for not collecting his nieces in Ciudad Juarez, then told him he must come to Columbus. "Nah, not Columbus, Ohio; Columbus, Nevada – to collect the girls. Tomorrow!"

"*Esta, quien es? Al diablo con estas niñas.* I not come to Columbus, Ohio OR Columbus, Nevada." He slammed down the receiver.

Happy gave me the look that told me she may have lost the first race on the racecard, but there were five more to go and she just might win one of the later ones. "Rick-Honey, Ah's got errands. Yo-all drahve to thet Palomas place."

Within an hour I was in the rental car with Happy's shopping loot: neat packages from a childrens' wear shop, and two bags with street-bought sandals. We'd had a french kiss, and Happy had waved me off. What was Happy going to do for the next ten hours? I'd never doubted Happy was a faithful wife. But, ten hours on her own in a strange town where she knew nobody. Why? She'd done her shopping.

Chapter 11

Puerto Palomas looked more cheerful in daylight.

The Dentistry building was less forbidding. Driving past it I recalled my terror as a four–year-old when my Dad took me to a dentist for the first time. I was as scared as a deer trapped by headlights.

I'd been right to be scared because that Warwickshire oaf had broken my loose baby tooth when he tried to pull it. God, but that had hurt.

Opposite the Dentistry, I saw a large furniture store. Maybe the Americans who came shopping across the border liked the handmade household goods and the prices here. I saw elaborate tin-framed mirrors displayed in the show window and hand-carved chairs painted in festive colors.

After my long, dry sprint, I was glad to pull in to the Bertha parking lot and head for its bar.

Oh, God no. Myra was there, eyes blazing and lips working. She grabbed my arm, and pulled me to one of the black enameled tables. She couldn't speak. She wrote on a napkin: "Anesthetic. Jaw numb. Can you see my new veneer job?" She opened her mouth, wide.

Myra was pulling at her numb jaw, using the index finger of her other hand to point to a shiny cap that most certainly was NOT the right color. Its bright pure virginal white contrasted dismally with her other yellowed teeth.

"Bring me a whisky," I said to the waiter. From her invitational sigh, I deduced Myra wanted one also. "Make that two."

We sat drinking in silence. This time Myra didn't plunge a hand into the bowl of peanuts. She shook her head in mock horror when I passed it in her direction. I remembered now it had been a peanut that dislodged her cap the night before.

I stared out at a playground beyond the bar's window. It had very little to keep kids quiet: an old-fashioned swing, and a see saw. There was no Jungle Jim or Bahamas slide.

There were no children playing.

No sight of Irina and the two other girls. I didn't finish my drink. I paid for both, and swung outside to explore the Pancho Villa grounds for other pursuits suitable for kids. There was a scruffy miniature golf area, too complicated for children of seven and nine.

And then I heard Myra screaming, baying, howling. The anesthetic added a ghastly weird tone to her cries.

I ran back toward the bar, but human traffic jostled and delayed any progress into the corridor beyond. The Pancho Villa Hotel guests were stampeding along with the hotel staff to peer down the long hall beyond the bar. Like at a bull fight or motor race, they were hoping to see that someone was killed: not a bullfighter or a racing driver, but a fellow guest.

They weren't disappointed. A bloodied male body lay crumpled there, like a pheasant shot to the ground.

He hadn't been shot. There was a large knife handle protruding from his anus.

Already a Mexican policeman was striding through the crowd. He had obviously been having a "quickee" with one of the local whores in a Pancho Villa Hotel bedroom. His pants were unzipped. And he wasn't wearing shoes.

He didn't lose the self-importance of a small town policeman. Quite efficiently he used the corridor chairs to create a blocked out crime scene.

I managed to employ my horseracing know-how to find light between the oglers and rushed to reach the corridor chairs.

Only half of the murdered victim's face was visible. I'd seen that half before. The man was Homburg hat. I'd seen him between two bottles of Listerine in the Ciudad Juarez Farmacia. I'd seen Irina's pictures of him taken on her mobile phone. He wasn't wearing his hat. And I hadn't seen his Maserati in the Pancho Villa Hotel parking lot. What had he been doing here? Alone? And without his car?

And Irina, and the two little girls? Why weren't they in this crowd of rubber-necking hotel guests?

Flashing blue lights: more police and an ambulance arrived.

Internationally accepted yellow tapes were strung from chair to chair to mark out the murder area. Now I saw the Homburg hat. It was sidelined, abandoned, on a chair.

Official photographs were taken. A forensic expert got busy. Fingerprints and DNA were lifted from the chairs nearest Irina's room. The door to her room had been opened by police orders, but found to be empty. Stripped of any sign of its latest occupants.

Myra, whose anesthetic was wearing off, jostled me and unasked translated orders barked by the more imposing of the policemen.

"He's asking the reception clerk to dig out the victim's passport. It seems he was an American. Maybe he came to Palomas to have his teeth done, like me. Reception clerk swears he arrived by taxi in the middle of the night. Maybe he was running from the Mexican police to be extradited. Apparently he has a criminal record here in Mexico. But Mexican law says a person is guilty until proven innocent. Just the opposite of our American 'innocent until proven guilty.' He had been alloted a room down this corridor. Left a 'Don't Disturb' sign on his door. Ordered breakfast for 10 a.m., I don't guess he ate it. Look, the breakfast tray's still farther up, there, in the corridor. Cereal untouched. Maybe he came out into the corridor to collect his breakfast."

"Did you see the lady and two little girls from the room opposite where the body –"

"Sure. You mean that Russian, and the two small illegals? They hitched a ride to Nogales, about an hour ago."

"The Russian lady's name is Irina. The little girls are Angela, and Flor. Why would they go to Nogales? On my map, Nogales is across the border in Mexico, not far from Tucson. Why, Arizona?"

"I think that woman's a Russian spy. I'd been listening to her all morning. She was determined to hitch a ride. Up to some monkey business: I could see it in her face. Desperate. She was absolutely desperate to hitch a ride. I think Nogales was the only ride offered. Got a ride from a dirty old man. I know the type. I'll bet he was more interested in the little girls than in the Russian. That woman is past interesting any regular guy. In my opinion, your Irina's had too many guys of all sorts during a long career as a *puta*."

Extricating myself from Myra, I went outside to the forlorn empty seesaw. Standing next to it, I pulled out my iPhone and dialed Happy's number.

She took a helluva long time answering.

"Hi, ya, Rick-Honey. Did the girls like them dresses?"

"Happy, they aren't here. I came straight to the Pancho Villa, but no sign of them. Apparently, Irina hitched a ride for the three of them to a Mexican town called Nogales, over the border from Tucson."

"Thet be in A-riz-ona?"

"Yes. Listen carefully now. There has been a murder here. In front of Irina's room. I saw half of the victim's face. He was curled up like a fetus, on his side, a knife's handle protruding from his ass. I believe the victim was Homburg hat. Mexican police are going to take the body away in an ambulance after a forensic job. I've come away from the crowd of hotel guests to ask you if I should try to track Irina, or come straight back to Columbus to collect you?"

"Cain't take me anywheres until t'morrow. Got plans. 'N yo-all don't need t'track Irina. She done call me t'tell me she done re-served a room in a ho-tel in thet No-gal-es. Ah got me the tel'phone numbuh. Rick-Honey. Hurry back. Ah's got needs."

My rental car was blocked by new arrivals, now probably milling about in the corridor taking iPhone pictures of the messy scene. No chance I could weed out the owners of the two cars blocking me: I decided to learn more about the why and how of Homburg hat's murder.

I began my inquiries in the bar. It was deserted. All the paying customers were still enjoying the free show in the corridor. The waiter had joined them, but the bartender was at his job polishing glasses. I took a stool and leaned my elbows on the bar.

"What it'll be?" he asked, with a faint trace of Polish accent. "Another whisky? Try a mojito?"

"Whisky and soda." Soda, because I didn't trust Mexico's water. "Tell me, did the murdered man come in here for a drink?"

"Sure. Nobody else working at three a.m. Only me, and old Juan who gives out keys to late nighters. Guest wore an old-fashioned hat. Were those called Homburgs? Wanted champagne, a mimosa. I didn't like to crack open a bottle just for one mimosa. But then the guy put a fifty dollar bill on the cash register's base. He told me: 'I want a lay.'

I'd replied: 'We have only one resident girl who might have obliged. But she's already got a policeman in her room."

I nodded. "Yes, I saw that policeman with his fly unzipped, and wearing no shoes. He got on *this case in a hurry."*

"That 3 a.m. customer turned grumpy. Snarled at me: 'Didn't say I wanted a girl. Want a boy.' And from the way a knife was sent to tear up his intestines from behind, I'll bet what he found was a Mexican kid with a very long knife. These Mexicans don't want to be taken for *maricones*."

"You heard nothing? No yell for help from the corridor? No thump when his body hit the tile?"

"Heard nothing."

"Don't you think you should tell the police about him asking for a rent-boy?"

"No way. I don't owe the Mexican police any favors. Want another whisky?"

"I don't think I'd better. Need to drive back to Columbus to my wife. Tell me, do you remember the blond woman who was with us last night? Russian accent?"

"You mean, the whore? She was wasting her talents here. Too old. Must be pushing sixty."

"I think she's closer to forty."

"Next time you see her, take a closer look. None of the American turistas would be interested. Too over the hill, her tricks were pathetic. I know an old whore when I see one: they never give up. Like actresses and singers, they think they can spin the magic even after sixty. Can't. Here in Mexico, men want them young. Younger all the time. No, that old whore couldn't get anyone to drive her and those kids out of here. Took hours of wiggling her tits to find a old guy who offered Nogales. She won't get any business there either. I guarantee it."

"How about Coyotes? I'd like to know if that late arrival asked to meet with Coyotes!"

"Nope. Rent boy. Only wanted a rent boy."

Without a comment I paid for my drink, and slipped out of the hotel to the car park. One of the cars had left that had been blocking my exit. Like a race car competitor at Le Mans, I wriggled the rental car out of its tight squeeze.

The Mexican ambulance left at the same time, its siren blaring.

Chapter 12

The next morning, without a word about what she'd been up to the day before, Happy was primed to leave for Nogales. I paid for our sex-blessed room, carried Happy's purchases to our rental car, and drove to a filling station to top up its tank with enough gasoline to make the trip to Tucson.

Highway 83 turned out to gift us with several scenic sights. We passed the Sahuaro National Park, with its display of those huge cacti with their uplifted arms. We viewed the distant Rincon Mountains. We raced parallel to a befuddled deer.

By the time we reached Tucson and found the hotel that Happy had chosen from her search on Google, I was more than ready to have a reprise of lovemaking.

From the terrace of our hotel bedroom we watched a glorious sunset that painted the Catalina Mountains a magical scarlet and pink. I took Happy into my arms and led her to the double bed from which we could follow that sunset into the deep blue of night.

In the early morning, we helped ourselves to the free breakfast, filled the car with petrol again, and got a map for the trip to Nogales. We headed out by Route 19, the quickest way from Tucson.

My iPhone's GPS did its thing again to point us to the outstanding architectural jewel of the region. We found ourselves reaching the graceful Spanish Mission Church called San Xavier. Happy said: "Slow down, Rick-Honey. Ah wants t'git a good looksee at thet theah church. Ah's sho thet Irina will wanna come visit the place."

Route 19 led us past two sets of mountains. Early on we had the Santa Rita range on the left. We passed the second range before we noticed the Sierrita Mountains were there on our right.

Entering Nogales, I punched my GPS to lead us to the El Regis Bar. I reckoned I could get a decent whisky there: a guide book had alerted me to the fact that American tourists preferred it. More importantly, Irina had used her mobile to suggest we meet there.

"*Da*! It located is in Hotel Regis, that has playground for the girls," she'd told Happy. "My hotel no amenities has. Quite awful place. You will see."

We'd had no trouble passing the U.S.A.-Mexico border. We'd changed places a few miles back: Happy thought it best for her to be in the driver's seat because she had an American passport. Our Ciudad Juarez rental car had Mexico plates, but Happy's American passport promised a quick pass-through. One look at my British neck-long haircut, and the border police reckoned I was a crazy jazz musician.

A Mexico border policeman asked Happy if she had Mexican insurance for the car. He spoke good English but had difficulty understanding Happy's Kentucky accent. "Sho do, off'suh."

Happy showed him the rental car's papers, and we were waved into Nogales, Mexico.

She took Calle San José, because she never relied on a GPS. Eventually, having careened through Avenida Juarez, the façade of El Rey Hotel loomed in front of us. Happy parked the car. I unloaded the girls' dresses and the last-minute Tucson purchase of a skirt for Irina.

The two girls saw us first. They ran to us, Angela acting slightly shy, not touching Happy, while Flor accepted Happy's motherly hug. Irina looked wan, worn-out. I thought: "Maybe she IS sixty, and it's too much of a chore to take care of two little girls."

Irina led us into the lobby. The girls wanted to peer into their packages. They tore open the matching cardboard boxes. Angela pulled out the tissue paper wrappings from inside and folded them neatly for another day. Flor saved the tissue paper but speedily hung her dress in the light from a picture window. Irina smiled gratitude, but left her present unopened, preferring to view it in private.

Tears vanished from Flor's face. For the first time it was wreathed with smiles. She was thrilled with the organdy party dress. Obviously she'd never had a party dress. In Spanish, she said: "*Quiero mostrar mi vestido a mi Mama.*" Irina translated for Flor: "I want to show my dress to my Mother." Angela said nothing: she stared at her dress's organdy ruffles that created a silk waterfall all the way to its hem. She ran her fingers ecstatically over the silk. I reckoned that it could be the first dress she'd ever had that was so fine, and not a hand-me-down.

Happy felt delighted that the girls were pleased with what she'd bought in Columbus. "Lets us'n go to yonder playground. Want fruit juice? Ap-ple juice?"

This hotel was adapted for child guests. There was a whirligig to take them on a round-the-circle ride like a merry-go-round without horses. A wading pool for tots had a lifeguard on duty. Two additional lifeguards watched swimmers in the heated pool. There was a soda fountain with light edibles. Happy, well-experienced on the subject of ever-hungry children, bought hamburgers and potato chips for the girls.

After tipping the unnecessary lifeguard supervising the un-used wading pool with a request in Spanish to keep a watch on the girls, Irina led us into the dark recesses of the Regis Bar. It was packed with the usual assortment of American *turistas*; the shoppers, the dentistry patients, and the boozers.

Shoppers were showing off what they'd purchased in stores and stalls near the hotel. They'd found much more variety here than we'd seen in Palomas or Ciudad Juarez. From what I'd seen in these narrow, zigzagged streets this was a Mecca for buyers of cheap goods, and probably for recreational drugs.

Shopping. One of Happy's favorite words. "Ah's sho goin' t'do some shoppin', Irina." Happy, well accustomed to perching on racehorses' saddles, had climbed astride a tall stool. There were four such stools around tables scattered haphazardly in the bar room. Irina and I had also climbed on stools. Happy, in a strange mood, with eyes alight, continued: "But furst, Ah wants t'hear how yo-all came heah."

If whores can blush, Irina blushed. There were more perspiration and red splotches all over her face. Her usual stink had intensified. My deodorant hadn't worked, or been left behind. "I got man to drive us here. Myra told me there were cheap hotels in Nogales. I found one with a double bed for $23 a night. Including cot for Flor."

"Don't none suhprise me it weren't up t'much. How'd yo-all git rid o' the man wut drove the cah?"

More perspiration spotted Irina's face. Like miniature wet beads the perspiration spread from her nose to her ears. "Paid him off."

Happy didn't prod further. She didn't want to know the details. She tried a different tack: "How'd yo-all git him outta the door." Happy ended lamely, "Later."

Had Happy told Irina about the murder in the corridor outside her room at The Hotel Bertha?

When Irina telephoned Happy to tell her she'd left Palomas for Nogales, did Irina explain WHY she'd left?

Perspiration dripped from the end of Irina's nose. "I use gambit learned in my early days. While he sat on the double bed, I asked him if he had read books by Dostoyevsky. No, he had not. Turganiev? No. Byelinsky? No. He cursed and called me a – what Americans say--- blue stocking? He storm out of room. I called the girls back from seesaws, and we were able go asleep."

"Let's us'n go shoppin'," Happy bit out the words. Suddenly, shopping wasn't a glorious event, it was a bittersweet maneuver to stop Irina's miserable flow. Happy didn't want to hear any more about the man who'd given Irina her "free" ride to Nogales.

"*Nyet.* Tired, exhausted. I cannot. *Spasive*, let me use the room you hire here. I need to nap." Irina's face sagged more. Like a sick swan's, her head rested on the front of her neck.

"Sho 'nuf. Yo-all go right ahead. Rick'll get the room."

I paid the bar bill, unable to put it on our room's account because I hadn't yet checked in. The three of us went to the reception clerk's desk. This time we didn't receive a cocked eyebrow: we had luggage, because Happy had made the rounds of shops and stalls in Columbus.

"Would Mrs. Harrow like to be serenaded? Mariachis would be an extra $100." The clerk murmured.

He gave me an-up-and–down look, stopping at my ring finger to see if I had a wedding band. Another up-and-down-look for Irina, and I could guess from his slight sneer that he had judged rightly she'd been a whore. Did he think I was planning to have a threesome?

A bellboy was summoned by a sharp, noisy bell. He looked sullen, pulling at the too-tight jacket that had obviously been bought for a smaller employee. He reminded me of a disgruntled New Boy at Eton, whose parents had bought his jacket second hand.

Happy kissed Irina lightly, and handed her a ceramic donkey purchased in Columbus. Irina, faded from want of sleep, barely acknowledged the gift. I gave her a slight wave. Happy took a quick peek at the outside playground to check that the girls were happily occupied. The lifeguard had handed them each a badminton racket and was giving a lesson on how to hit the feathered cock. Relieved that they were being cared for, Happy gave me a thumbs-up and we left the lobby to stroll down the Calle San José.

We spent an hour exploring the stores and outdoor stalls. Their prices didn't magnetize us; they'd been inflated for the turistas.

"Rick-Honey, wut yo-all think o' the Mexican China Poblana skirts fo' the girls? Ah loves all them sequins, 'n red go fahne with the green."

"I doubt they'll be going to any costume party soon."

"Cain't be so sho. Thet cranky ole' uncle in Chi-ca-go may yet come fo' the girls." She bought the costume's blouse but not the skirt for Angela, recalling that her miniskirt had been a turn-down. Happy chose a doll dressed in the china poblana costume for Flor. For Irina she chose a large porcelain plate with a hand-painted eagle in flight.

"Darling, aren't you going to buy anything for yourself?"

"Sho am. Lookee in thet there jeweler-man's window. Ah lahkes all them tur-quoise things. The bra-ce-lets. Rings. Earrin's. But if it ain't too 'spensive, Ah's gonna git me thet belt. Nevuh had no belt studded with tur-quoises."

I gave a short laugh, but pulled out my credit card. "I don't think your racing valet will let you wear it. And it probably weighs a lot. That would throw off your ride's published weight."

"Ain't plannin' t'wear it racin'; thought Ah'd make an entrance wearin' it next time yo-all in-vites me to dinner at Claridge's." She echoed my short laugh. We gave the jewelry store a miss.

Turning back towards the El Rey, still on Avenida Juarez, we stopped at a huge plate glass window crammed with silver, hammered in a Mexican style. There were ashtrays, candlesticks, large platters, individual serving plates; the lot to dandy-up any home. Without a word, Happy pranced into the shop to leave minutes later with an oblong platter. "This be fo' both o' us. Fo' ourn house in Epsom."

With that elated feeling of having made a good purchase at a fair price, we lingered in front of two more windows before Happy looked at her watch. "Yo-all think thet lifeguard still be watchin' the girls?"

We cut short the window gazing. Happy, totally fixated on her purchase, almost tumbled a fat turista whose eyeglasses went flying.

Happy was breathless when we re-entered the El Rey's lobby. Angela and Flor were seated primly in twin chairs near the hall porter's desk. Happy's shoulders bucked with relief. She hugged both of the children. Both were holding on carefully to their new dresses, although Flor's had already fallen in the playground's dust.

"Irina?" Happy gestured toward the single elevator. Angela understood. She shook her head. *"No hemos vista su amiga,"* which Happy correctly guessed meant that Angela had not seen Irina.

Happy held on to the blouse and doll she'd bought. I imagine she felt that they'd had enough presents for one day. She'd save those for tomorrow.

I asked the hall porter for a duplicate key, and added: "What floor?"

"Fifth. Your room is number thirteen." The hall porter put out her palm for a tip. I gave her two U.S. dollars: I thought that was enough for such a brief reply.

Happy asked: "From what time do they serve children's dinners?"

"Six o'clock."

She slipped her a dollar without her having extended the palm again.

We buzzed for the elevator. It stopped at floors Two, Three, and Four before its rattling door emptied it of passengers. It was an extremely narrow elevator. I wondered how hotel guests could fit in suitcases they didn't want to entrust to a bell boy. Did the hotel have a separate elevator for suitcases?

I had no need of a key. Room thirteen's door opened without one. Playing the gentleman, I let Happy go in first.

She gave a gasp, a cry, and then a whimper. "Get the chillun away; don't let 'em see."

I saw. Before herding the two girls down to two chairs in the corridor, I'd seen, horrified, Irina's body where it lay on our double bed. Her knees had been cocked, and spread wide apart: a knife's hilt stuck out from between them. There was more blood in that bed than if she'd just given birth to a baby. But it was murder, not new life that had crimsoned those sheets.

Chapter 13

Calming the little girls' curiosity, "I said; "Irina's sleeping." I put my two hands together next to my right ear in the international sign meaning asleep. I tried a new gambit, I gestured at the new dresses and tried to get over to them that I wanted both girls to put these on. Give me a fashion show.

Ashen, Happy emerged into the corridor. She caught on to what I was up to. Quickly, she shoved the girls into a linen cupboard with their new dresses, up buttoned this new finery, and added her own touch. She unwrapped two headscarves from her handbag, fitted one on to the top of each curly black head, then turned to me as she re-emerged into the corridor: "Rick," she hadn't enough breath to add her habitual Honey. "Gimme them car keys. We's runnin' down them back stairs to the car pahk. Keep yourn iPhone tuhned on. Ah'll let yo-all know wheah we gone."

I was left to deal with stashing the girls' El Paso convent uniforms under a bale of dirty linen. Returning to the corpse, I used the house phone from the night stand to inform Reception that there was a dead woman in our bed. While speaking, I noticed that Irina's mobile phone was on the night stand. I pocketed it, pushed it deep down beside my iPhone. I didn't savor having Irina's death connected to yesterday's murder in Palomas. Homburg hat's portrait, and the later picture of him in the Maserati, were still both on that mobile phone.

I heard the receptionist hollering down an outside line. I guessed she was speaking to local police. I hadn't understood a word of what was said, but managed to do the essentials during the few minutes left to me before the expected tsunami of *policia* entered our room.

First things first. I looked for something I could use that would mask my fingerprints. I found paper bags for the disposal of tampax and kotex. Grabbing two, I fitted one over the handle of the very bloodied knife protruding from between Irina's legs. I pulled out the knife, taking care to wrestle hard with its handle to make sure it didn't slip out of its bag. Holding that bag in my left hand, I used my right to raise up the air-conditioning's grill and pushed the knife and its bag inside the air-conditioning's tube. I replaced the grill, and strode back to the bed. Covering my right hand with the remaining opened bag, I used both hands to gently shove down one and then the other of Irina's knees to rest on the bottom sheet.

The hotel manager, the police, the coroner could imagine whatever: that she'd lost a baby through miscarriage, she'd had a menopausal hemorrhage, or she'd had an unusually heavy period. At first sight, now Irina's bloodied legs did not necessarily shout MURDER.

A cursory examination by a hotel doctor, being urged by the hotel manager to reduce the impact of what had happened that day with a view to keeping this out of the newspapers, would possibly serve for the HUSH-UP I wanted.

When the manager, doctor and a policeman – all of whose afternoon work had been interrupted – broke into our room, I had my story prepared.

I knew better than to give different stories, particularly to police.

"You are Señor Richard Harrow? English? Race horse trainer?" I nodded to the policeman.

These facts I'd written on the hotel registration form.

I put on my 'lost a race face' to show sympathy for Irina's passing, but made sure I kept my emotions low key.

"Home address?"

"Harrow Racing Stables, Epsom, England."

"How long do you intend to remain in Mexico?"

"Three days." I pulled out my airline tickets. They had our return date.

"*El CAPITAL.* You will be returning to Mexico City to take your flight?"

"Certainly."

"Why did you come to Nogales?"

Now I skirted the truth, still keeping to facts "My wife likes to shop. She'd heard there were bargains in hammered silver here. You can check out that we bought a silver platter in the store two blocks from the hotel. I paid for it by credit card. You will see my name on the shop's copy."

"How long have you known the deceased?"

"Let me think . . . Three days."

"Only three days? And you let her sleep in your bed!"

"My wife is generous-hearted. She liked this woman. She made the offer when Irina said she felt extremely tired."

The hotel doctor had been nodding his head. Suddenly, he stopped nodding, straightened his back from where he'd been examining Irina's re-opened legs.

He spat out a flow of curses. I recognized one highly punctuated phrase: *"Esto no es normal."*

NORMAL. That word had the same weighted meaning in Spanish or English.

I directed myself to the Hotel Manager. My aim was to put on a plausible act that could permit me to exit the room.

"I'd scarcely known Irina. We met three days ago in Ciudad Juarez. She'd traveled in the same bus. Irina translated for my wife. Irina's Spanish was good, she must have lived in Mexico for some time. Helped me too, because neither my wife nor I speak Spanish, and this poor soul was fluent in your language."

"What was her family name?"

"No idea. We only knew her as Irina."

"Her nationality?"

"Russian. I believe she'd told my wife she'd been born in Leningrad. Called St. Petersburg, now, again."

"Do you know if she checked into another hotel?"

"Yes. I believe she did. Or so she said in a telephone call to my wife. I don't recall that she told her its name. She met us here in this hotel for a drink. She'd been babysitting two little girls my wife wanted to help. As I've said, the lady complained she felt terribly tired. So my wife offered to let her take a nap in our bed."

My old father, in Warwickshire, had always advised: "Keep to the truth." And when I was in the army my regiment's smart guy advised: "Never volunteer information."

The repeated use of "my wife" got me into trouble.

"WHERE *is* your wife?" The policeman interrupted. He'd been examining Irina's private parts at the doctor's instigation. He got out his mobile phone. Oh, oh. I knew that modern technology had arrived to connect policemens' mobiles -- even Mexican policemens' mobiles -- to computors with the latest information.

How long before this policeman connected the dots concerning yesterday's knifing in Palomas, and this Russian woman's death?

Where WAS Happy? Had she finally tried to cross the U.S. border with those two little girls?

I needed to get out of that room, out of that hotel. I needed to use my iPhone to call Happy.

The dire situation deterioraed into something worthy of a TV reality show. I stood quietly trapped while the Hotel Manager complained that this room's bed and sheets had been ruined. He didn't say that their replacement cost would be added to my bill. I hastened to offer to pay whatever that would cost, and then forcefully brought up the subject of my prompt departure.

Without waiting for more trouble, I walked to where the bell boy had parked our two suitcases, took them in hand, and walked out the door.

None of the three stopped me. I took the elevator to the lobby and checked the bar for Happy. No sign of her, but the bartender had a word for me. "When you check out, don't forget my tip."

His tip! As if I didn't have enough on my mind. I paid for one night's stay, although we hadn't spent five minutes together in that room. I went into the car park to call Happy. I DID have more pressing things on my mind!

Amazing, how the trivia of everyday life intruded on the big, grisly events.

I connected to Happy's iPhone. Happy's voice was like a balm on a suppurating sore. "Hi, Rick-Honey. We'uns be casin' thet ho-tel o' Irina's. Angela remembuhed the name and showed me how t'git theah. Ah's needed to clar'fy mah mind. Po'r Irina! Weren't nothin' Ah c'd do fo' Irina at ourn ho-tel."

"Give me the name. I'll jump in a cab."

"Nah, don't. It be called Cloister. Re-ligious name, but no place fo' nuns. Bad nei'bor-hood. Hidden be-tween shacks fo' houses. But

Ah's learned me wut Ah's needed t'know." Deep breath. "The 'dirty ole guy' wut drove huh t'Nogales. He din't kill Irina. He be sittin' in the Cloister's Coffee Shop fo' the last hour, waitin' fo' Irina to come outta huh room. She'd sneaked away t'meet usn at the EL REY. Ah's leavin' this place now. Meet me behind the shop wheah we'uns bought the silvuh dish. But keep yourn haid down. Ah's got somepin' REAL strange t'tell yo-all."

"Tell me NOW."

"Naw. Ah knows yo-all. Darlin' there'd be no way yo-all w'd stop tryin' t'be a he-ro. Ah luvs mah husb'nd. Don't wanna be no widaw lady. Puh-leese, meet me b'hind thet silvuh shop."

No arguing with Happy! Why would she become a widow if I caught a cab to the Cloister Hotel? What could have made Happy think that 'the ole man' who drove Irina to Nogales might have murdered Homburg hat, AND Irina?

With the two suitcases slapping at my ankles, I switched from taking the obvious, short few-blocks route along Avenida San José. There was one plus, there were ramshackle hovels hovering over a side street, offering cover like a grove of low branched trees at a boar shoot.

I gave a deep sigh of relief when Happy parked our rental car behind one of the hovels. Very speedily I packed in our two suitcases. I kissed my wife and gave her hips a blunt shove to take over the driver's seat. Neither of us said a word: there was too much of importance to say. Like gold medal Olympic athletes, we needed to be in a private place to chat. Not expose information in public. The 'how I did it' wasn't to be repeated; the gold medalists weren't liable to give away what earned them a gold instead of silver. Sharp shooting Olympic champion Carola Mandel always alleged that the Russian team had studied her every move, *practiced* her moves, and that was why the Russian team displaced her and took the gold four years later.

WHAT was it that Happy wanted to save for pillow talk?

Both of our little girl passengers marked my return by making cheerful sounds that must have meant 'Glad to see you back,' in Spanish.

I gave them a 'hello' wave, but concentrated on my exit from Nogales. "Where are we headed?" I asked Happy.

She had the GPS already programmed. It read CENTRAL TIJUANA.

Chapter 14

When we hit the main highway leading due West, Happy finally confided her big news. It wasn't dampened by the amazing sight of the border's steel walls stretching to the horizon. "Ah's seen the Maserati."

"But Homburg hat's dead!"

"Sho 'nuf. But Homburg hat, he be a chau-ffeur. He nevuh owned thet car."

"Did you see if there was a passenger?"

"Nah. They ain't been none. Just 'nothuh chau-ffeur. Alone in the car. Same homo type lahke Homburg hat. Lahkely he favuhs boys too."

"Why are we going to Tijuana?"

"Ah wuz fillin' up ourn tank with gas 'n Ah sees thet Maserati at same pump. Ah's heard chau-ffeur men-tion Tijuana at the cashier's. He bought a map. Got hisself told wut h'way t'take."

"Happy, my darling. Our return tickets are only good if we fly back home in three days' time. We should be going to Mexico City. AND, we've got Angela and Flor to think about. When you took the car from El Rey, I thought you were heading to go across the U.S. border to deliver them to their uncle."

"Naw. No way. Ah's decided ag'in breakin' the law. Nevuh done it be-fo'. Well, once, only to grab some chewin' gum from a broken vendin' machine. 'N anyways their uncle won't have them. Gave me the fi-nal 'NO.' If'n AH got them into the U-nited States, these kids'd be put in some holdin' fa-ci-lity. Maybe fo' months. 'N then sent to Gua-te-mala by bus. Ah's goin' t'finish wut-all Ah's come to do. 'N then Ah's takin' these kids to Santa Elena to their Mamas. Wheah they belongs!"

"Santa Elena?"

"Yup. Remembuh thet theah lifeguard at El Rey? Well, Angela told the lifeguard thet huh Mama didn't have a phone. But thet huh Grandmama did, and thet she lived in Santa Elena. The lifeguard, he got the code fo' area o' Tikal. Ah's asked him to talk on mah iPhone to Flor's Gran Mama. He done told huh 'Me-ri-can lady's goin' t'bring Flor back home 'cause uncle not willin' t'take the girls. He put Flor on to speak to huh Gran Mama. Li'l Flor, she be as ex-cited as mah Dorothy when Ah phones huh Ah's comin' home."

"Good show. But Happy, you can't hope to finish what you contracted for. Now that we've seen the scope of the problem -- unaccompanied children in their thousands -- you'll have to find some way to get out of that contract with Hannibal. As for Angela and Flor going back to their mothers, how do you intend to get them to some obscure town in Guatemala?"

"Don't yo-all worry yourn haid, Rick-Honey. Ah's goin' t'straighten things out when we'uns gits t' Tijuana."

"Aren't you overlooking there's a murderer at large who has struck near us? And that this time YOU could be the target?"

"HE'S the one wut should worry. Ah's got him in mah sights."

Chapter 15

The border became uglier the closer we came to Tijuana. Now there was barbed wire topping the steel walls. Closed circuit TV cameras were strategically placed.

No privacy here! What I hated the most were the *dirt* detection roads that revealed illegals' footprints to help helicopters track them. There were road signs indicating a father, mother, and child running: like deer signs where deer might be on the road and damage a passing car. If this wasn't a war zone, it was still awful.

I thought of Germany's concentration camps in World War II and how an escapee would have been hunted down in much the same way.

We didn't talk much. We shared a sandwich, but were careful not to wake the two girls. Flor, for the first time since she'd joined us, had stopped her sporadic weeping. According to Happy, ever since Flor had spoken to her grandmother and been assured she'd be welcomed home, she'd come out of her chrysalis to grow butterfly wings.

Had the child believed she'd done something wicked to be sent away?

Tijuana's twenty-four-hour wild play dens emitted garish lights seen from miles away. We sped toward them out of the seemingly-eternal-desert darkness. We'd felt threatened for miles by stygian mountains looming next to the toll way like the ruins of 9/11's downed skyscrapers.

Happy, who has proven to be very adept at milking her iPhone, had searched Google for a list of mid-priced hotels. She'd decided on the Como, at $59 a night for a double bed and two cots.

It was close to midnight when we drew up to its entrance. This time I had suitcases, which allayed suspicions of a one-night stand.

The unshaven receptionist accepted my credit card for pre-payment. He didn't give a second look at the two Guatemalan children accompanying two *Gringos*.

Our bedroom was on the main floor. Noisy, from raucous voices and loud music coming from a bar next door, we each gentled a child onto a cot, and then climbed into our queen-sized – not double –bed.

I couldn't sleep from worry, anxious what Happy would try when dawn came. I couldn't make love to my wife with two children within yards of us.

Chapter 16

Happy left after dawn for the U.S.A.

At the Tijuana-San Diego border crossing, Happy had all the necessary papers. When we'd been mugged in Mexico City and been thrown in that garbage dump, Happy had been left with her passport and driver's license. Now, trapped in a ragged line of cars awaiting their turns to show their papers, Happy had prepared hers in plenty of time before the Nissan finally slid up for inspection of the car and its occupant.

Happy produced each document as required. She wanted no last minute hitch. She showed the Mexican insurance policy I'd taken out on the Nissan in Ciudad Juarez. She held out the Nissan's rental papers: they were in order. Happy jotted down the officer's name, and the number on his badge. She wrote down the precise hour when she crossed.

"Off-i-cah," she purred, "Can Ah tu'n in this heah rent-al cah in A-meri-ca? Ah jus' maght wanna go back in t'Mex'co by bus. Cheapah. Or, mebbe someone will lend me a cah. Cain't say as Ah lahkes this one much."

The officer recognized her Kentucky hills drawl. "Don't know about Mexican rental cars. Say, are you from near Louisville? I've got a cousin in Louisville."

"Sho am. Got mah auntie 'n uncle in Louisville. Uncle, he be a hot walker at Chu'chill Downs."

With a friendly smile, the officer waved Happy into her homeland. "You'd better get going. There's quite a long line behind you. Fur million cross here."

Happy drove straight to where her iPhone's GPS located the City Hall. She paid into a meter for one hour to park the Nissan, then strode into what was a heavily guarded building to see the mayor.

She made it past the security guard, but was not so successful with the mayor's secretary. Intelligence shone from the woman's inquiring eyes. She was smartly dressed in a well-cut business suit in tangerine, with five inch heel shoes in a darker tone verging on brown. Happy still wore the T-shirt and jeans she'd slept in. There hadn't been time for a comb-out, her curls were bedraggled. On her feet she had the Ciudad Juarez flip flops. Happy's appearance was a far cry from the elegantly outfitted wife of a Trainer that she annually presented for Royal Ascot.

The secretary asked Happy what her business was with the mayor. "And do you have an appointment? I don't see a Mrs. Richard Harrow's name on his schedule."

"Nah. But Ah's got this!" Happy placed on the secretary's desk Irina's mobile, still encased in the tampax paper bag. "Evidence t'convict a murderuh 'n his boss, wut send him to kill folks."

"Please, leave. Leave, now!" The immaculate secretary's polite expression turned to disgust, then fury. She didn't know there was a mobile telephone inside the bag. It could have contained used tampons. She didn't want to have to touch the bag to remove it from her desk. She pointed to it, wordless, one perfectly manicured fingernail edging within inches of that offending tampax disposal bag.

Happy scooped it up. "Got me a mobile inside this-heah bag. Mobile wut got finguh prints 'n DNA of a murderuh. Please. It's impo'tant. Please, Ah needs t'see the ma-yor."

At the precise moment that Happy retrieved the mobile, a set of elegantly carved doors opened from within and two men walked past the secretary's desk. Both treated Happy as if she was invisible. She could have been a fly that had somehow managed to get into this air-conditioned building.

The shorter of the two men waved to the secretary. It was a so-long-for-now gesture. Happy guessed he was the mayor. She dove for him, but never got a chance to speak. His secretary, her poise regained, rose from her desk and propelled Happy through another set of doors that led to a service elevator.

Happy obediently buzzed for the elevator to collect her. There was a wait, and when the elevator door opened she could see there had been waste amassed from floors below. A neatly uniformed porter stood next to two full bins. He gave Happy a disparaging sneer, due to the condition of her clothes.

"'Nuf, Ah gits the me-ssage," At floor level, Happy left the elevator to search for a shop where she could buy fresh, suitable clothes. This time she didn't naggle over prices: she took the first clothes shown to her. She still had time on the parking meter to find a pair of shoes. She bought boots, ever mindful that she could put them to good use later.

The shopping revived Happy's spirits. Determined to achieve what she'd come to do, she returned to the Nissan and used her iPhone's GPS to show her the way to the Municipal Police Station.

Her iPhone's GPS complied.

She had barely enough coins for an hour on the nearest meter. Happy was feeding in the coins, concentrating on not wastefully spilling any onto the sidewalk, when strong fingers applied a chloroform-filled neckerchief to her nostrils. Simultaneously her open mouth was clamped like a goldminer's safe by another hand.

Within seconds, Happy passed out. Before slipping into total unconsciousness, she heard a concerned passerby asking, "Can I help? You have a phone? Shall I call 911 for you?"

Boris, Irina's murderer, ably replied: "My wife's pregnant and faints easily. I've got smelling salts for her."

When Happy recovered, she was in the Maserati's front seat. Her hands had been tied with the stinking neckerchief rolled into a makeshift rope. Her feet were bare; the new boots had been torn off. There was tape over her mouth.

A familiar voice from the rear of the car blew her mind.

She heard Hannibal say: "Got you, Happy Harrow. Now I have to think of an appropriate way to rid myself of you. Trampled by a racehorse? That could play well for an apprentice jockey. No, too much trouble to locate an available tantrum-prone horse. Let's see: a drowning? Type a suicide note and toss you from the Mezcala Bridge. Can you type? Forget that: too many people at all hours on that bridge."

Happy had one thought: "Who will take care of mah chillun?"

Hannibal droned on, evidently enjoying the sound of his own voice. "A crowd scene COULD be a good choice. San Diego's Festival of the Bikers starts tomorrow. Yes, I can get quite inventive for that."

Irina's murderer said nothing. Trained like a hound to obey a hunter's orders while remaining silent, Boris concentrated on driving. It would have been a crucial error to get stopped by a border policeman for speeding or changing lanes! But even a hound gets a chance to bay, if only to the moon.

And Boris got his chance. A border patrol officer stopped the Maserati. "You in there? What's this woman got her mouth taped for?"

Hastily Boris whined: "Accident."

Hannibal, enjoying this, took up the challenge. "Officer, may I have your name, and the numbers on your badge? Yes, and the license number of your patrol car, please. I will be telling the hospital that I took longer than expected to arrive due to your efforts. Only doing your duty, of course. But my maid had an accident with masking tape this morning, and I was told to bring her – as is – S.O.P. My driver, Boris, should have signaled before changing lanes. Forgive us, we're panicking, in such a hurry."

"Sorry, Sir. Sorry. We see all kinds of accidents, but this was a new one for me." He revved his patrol car's motor and drove away, while Hannibal chuckled with pleasure at his own inventiveness.

Happy felt no additional fear. She knew what she was dealing with. The super ego of this man had revealed itself to her during the past few days. She determined to stay alive, and to accomplish what needed to be done.

Hours later, hungry, and thirsty, Happy noted the approach of evening by crimson arcs of light that ventured through a crescent shaped window into the basement where she had been thrown.

She hoped the dinner hour might mean food and water, and -- most urgently -- the removal of the tape over her mouth.

Happy had been marched into a Hollywood 1930s-style mansion. It had a basement. It was in the basement that she was now bound to a chair.

When she sign-languaged to Boris that she MUST go to a toilet or soil the basement floor, he unbound her legs, returned the boots and pushed her into the cubicle, then watched her pee with a lascivious smirk.

Happy had been stripped of her handbag while still in the Maserati. There had been a great business of searching for Irina's mobile, both Hannibal and Boris apparently very aware of the photographs that were in it. But, strangely for murderers, it seemed they had not ascertained the mobile's ownership. The late Homburg hat had mentioned the photo session in the Farmacia. He had not specified that it was Irina who owned the mobile.

Chapter 17

Boris was not going to miss dinner. When night was fully upon them, he left Happy alone, in the light of a large antique chandelier with one single bulb standing tall like a spacecraft on its launching pad.

Surreptitiously, Happy felt for her own iPhone. It was held in her armpit by the strap of her bra. Checking to ascertain that it was still fully charged, she debated whether to use it to call me, or the police, or to use a text message. She discarded the first idea because her mouth was taped closed and also she didn't want her captors to hear her speaking even in garbled words.

She sent me a text message.

Happy, who had taken diction lessons to correct her Kentucky hills' fracture of the English language, had long ago decided that she was going to speak like her Auntie Mae did. When she wrote, however, she took immense care to use the right word and to spell correctly, but used foreshortened words *à la* text messages.

This is what my Happy put in her text, which meant that I got it as she wrote it.

From: H. Harrow, Harrow Racing Stables, Epsom, Surrey UK To: Rick Harrow, Harrow Racing Stables, Epsom, Surrey UK

Dear Rick, Hannibal Kash ordered his driver Boris to kill Irina, because Irina was with us on trip from Mexico City, and witness when Coyote arrived at terminal and collected busload of illegals. As u recall, Irina went into Ciudad Juarez with u to buy goods at drugstore and there found Hannibal hat. Flirting, Irina handed her mobile to Homburg hat for him to take selfie. Vain, he swallowed bait. He left DNA and fingerprints on mobile. Selfie photo good likeness. But when u gave all this incriminating material to the local police, they not arrest him, because u saw him later buying liquor at a store. I had strange telephone call from Hannibal Kash later, where he changed his original orders to me, telling me I was not to involve myself with any Coyotes. Incredibly, for such a rich man, he complained to me that the Coyotes tripled prices from $7000 to $21,000. Not for illegals to pay that. For Hannibal to pay THEM. Hannibal was PAYING Coyotes, not having them ARRESTED. Boris is current driver 4 Hannibal. Boris killed Homburg hat in Puerto Palomas, Boris killed Irina in Nogales. Irina murdered when she made connection between Homburg hat and Hannibal. I am at present held by Hannibal and Boris in basement of mansion in San Diego. Hannibal boasted he would have Boris kill me during Festival of the Bikers in Golden Gate Park. I believe Hannibal's Maserati parked in circular drive of house where I am held. If u locate Maserati u will have found me. HELP! I am the mother of our three children, who need me. Hillary "Happy" Harrow

Chapter 18

I hadn't been able to sleep. The two little girls got up twice for water and then I had to tuck them into their cots again.

There was no wifely soft, cuddly body for me to warm up to.

I'd checked my iPhone every hour hoping to connect with Happy. After I received her long text message, I immediately forwarded the salient parts to the San Diego police and MI6. As it is not that difficult to forward texts, I sent my Head Groom, dear old Tom, a copy of her full text. I also managed to send the text to dear Elga.

Nothing more from Happy. I phoned her, and got a very angry Happy growling through a taped mouth: "Ring off." The fact that her voice sounded feisty cheered me somewhat, but I couldn't put my mind around what I should do. There I was, in Tijuana, with no car and two little illegals who had come to depend on the Harrows. I couldn't leave two girls, seven and nine, alone. Not in Tijuana, ranked as the eighth most evil city on the planet.

I knew in my gut we needed helicopters to find Happy. Had the San Diego police department received Happy's text I'd relayed, believed it, acted on it? Surely the police could scramble helicopters. Weathermen fly in them at all hours. Damn, saving my wife should have priority over knowing whether or not it's going to rain. I unplugged my iPhone from its charger, locked myself in the bathroom for privacy, got on to Information, dialed the number for San Diego's main police station and introduced myself.

"Yes. Harrow. Spelt like the school. No, not being funny, there is a well-known school called Harrow in England. First name, Richard. Pull up my particulars on the internet. I am a racehorse trainer. Based in Epsom, Surrey, with the same address on the e-mail you have seen and thought it a hoax. No, I'm British, but my wife IS an American citizen. Yes, she lives in England, usually, but she'd been contracted to make a study of what you call the Coyotes who transport illegals across the border. We planned to leave for London in three days, the job didn't work out. She is in real danger. The men, who have her now, killed a driver and a Russian woman this very week: exactly as described by my wife in her text. And have you Googled to learn about my wife? You'll learn that she is the sleuth who unmasked seven serial killers. Please, if you can't discuss this case, put your superior officer on the phone."

No go.

There followed a long period of waiting while listening to the banter in a police station, cups of coffee being set on the table next to the phone, many landlines ringing, gruff voices shouting. Finally my request for a supervisor was honored and a gruff voice came on the line. "Give us a description of your wife. Height, age, weight, color of hair, eyes. Any distinguishing marks?"

"Height, five feet one; age, twenty-six; weight, one eighteen; hair blonde, eyes crystal blue. But I can do better. She won a horse race in Japan three years ago: there were photos of her in the newspapers, picked up on the internet.'

A pause. He was Googling Happy's win in Kyoto. "I see her photograph. What was she wearing today? Anything noteworthy?"

"She left Tijuana this morning in a T-shirt and jeans. Don't count on her to still be in those. My wife loves shopping. She probably nipped into a San Diego shop for something more citified. Please, do you have a helicopter available? Start searching for that damn Maserati!"

"You won't be permitted to go up in a police helicopter, Mr. Harrow. If that's what you want."

"I want my wife back safe and sound. There's more hideous detail in this case. The man who actually does the killing is a sadist. Disembowels the victim, via one orifice or another. For God's sake, is my wife to be next, while we waste time talking?"

The serious voice, no name given, tried to pacify. "We'll be doing the best we can. But, you're right: no more talk. I've got to get going."

Throwing on my jeans and T-shirt, I packed up my few possessions, woke up the little girls, told them to hurry dressing, and tried once again to wrap my mind around the situation. I put all my mental energy to work, and finally a thought rose like a phoenix.

"NUNS!" I said aloud.

Angela and Flor emerged from the bathroom to stare. They hadn't understood. Their knowledge of the English language had extended to the 'Please' and 'Thank you' we'd instilled into our own kids. "Nuns" was still foreign.

They began what was now a daily ritual. Angela changed Flor's band aids. Flor drew the lice eggs comb through Angela's hair.

I unpacked my iPhone and dialed the Ciudad Juarez number that had been wonderfully helpful earlier. Mother Antonia answered.

"Mr. Harrow? How nice to hear from you. How are you, your wife, and the two little illegals?"

"Desperate for your help! Angela and Flor are all right, here with me now but going home to their mothers in Guatemala. Reverend Mother, Irina was murdered, yesterday, in Nogales. My wife Is being held by her killer. Across the border, in San Diego. I need to go there to push the police to find her before she --."

"Where are you now? And, how can I help?"

"Tijuana. Mother Antonia, I remembered how you found two discarded convent uniforms for Angela and Flor. Please, I pray to God, you could call around to a few convents to find a nun in Tijuana to take the girls while I rush to San Diego."

"I do know several nuns in Tijuana. Give me your iPhone number and I will call you back when I have a positive answer. Poor Irina! So ecstatic about our churches here! When all is resolved, we shall have a Memorial Service for her. Your number, Mr. Harrow?"

I gave it. I led the girls to the breakfast lounge. Before they had finished their *huevos con jamon*, my iPhone rang.

"Mr. Harrow? I know the urgency you are under. I will be brief. Go to the Convent School in the Matanzas barrio. Ask for the Mother Superior. Her name? Sister Benedicta. She's well known for taking in illegals. She knows your whole story. God speed."

I paid the hotel bill. There was a hiccup. Happy had sent the organdy party dresses to be dry-cleaned and the two girls wailed when I told them we'd have to leave the dresses behind. Finally, when there was a delay in getting a taxi, the dresses duly arrived, exquisitely wrapped.

I paid off the dry cleaner's delivery man, handed each girl her dress in its long bag, and all was calm again.

Our taxi driver knew the location of the convent in the Matanzas barrio. Like a father grouse who protects his chicks by luring a predatory hawk in an opposite direction from his mate, our driver skillfully lost an overly inquisitive Cadillac. It had veered too close several times to case this driver's passengers.

A Coyote?

Sister Benedicta left a class of choral singers to greet us. We could hear the words of these children's cheerful song wafting into the street like seagulls on salt air: "Ave, Ave, Ave Maria."

This was a nun experienced in the ways of Latin American children. After she introduced herself in Spanish to Angela and Flor, she complemented them on their beautifully wrapped party dresses. She gathered the dresses with consummate care, expertly handling these two little girls far from home.

I wasn't exactly abrupt, but I didn't have time to enter into a polite conversation with her. As I knew she knew the dire threat facing my absent wife, I didn't need to give any explanation. I hugged Angela and Flor, and promised that I would return to take them to their Mamas.

The taxi driver had waited for me, and with his broken English and my total lack of any words in Spanish we somehow struck a bargain. He would drive me to the Golden Hill Park mentioned in Happy's e-mail. *If* I agreed to pay a return fare.

I agreed.

The border crossing wasn't as difficult as I'd imagined. Apparently there is a law which permits a person of any nationality to go to San Diego for one day. Registered taxis, with their car papers and insurance up to date, ply back and forth. My driver had a clean slate. Sister Benedicta had chosen well.

My driver rolled into Golden Gate Park at the same time as police helicopters began whirling overhead.

A bad sign.

There would have been no helicopters if Happy had been freed.

My eyes left the helicopters to study the surroundings. What must have been designed for peaceful hours of contemplation viewing magnificent panoramas and a stunning landscape, was an incredible mess. Clumps of half-naked men with helmets were coddling mountain bikes. Some had removed the tires for closer inspections, or re-assembled their wheels' chains. I caught two bikers peeing against the park's trees. MAYBE THERE WEREN'T ENOUGH PUBLIC TOILETS, OR MAYBE THESE BIKERS DIDN'T TRUST THE PUBLIC NOT TO STEAL THEIR BIKES.

Vendors of fairground goodies moved among them to eke out money from these men who had stripped themselves and their bikes to the barest necessities. "Agua, Agua," called a stooped cripple, who made me think of Hugo's HUNCHBACK OF NOTRE DAME. But, *where* was Esmeralda?

No sign of my wife.

I wasn't hungry, however I considered that my driver had eaten nothing. Gesturing toward a stand with a banner spelling: TAQUERIA, by sign language I offered to treat him to whatever he fancied.

And then I saw Happy.

She came, weaving through the groups of bikers, sandwiched between Hannibal and his new chauffeur, named in Happy's text as Boris! Her face looked extremely pale, but I saw in her eyes a determination to stay alive. I noticed that the area around her mouth showed a redness due to having tape pulled off the skin. Strips of skin were missing from her wrists and ankles, in some of these places there was blood.

Not one of the three had seen me.

I wanted to kill Hannibal, slaughter Boris. A rage like I'd never felt before surged burning into my deepest being. How COULD I have left my darling wife to be captured by such as these! The rage was against myself.

Calm down.

Think.

It wouldn't help Happy for me to go flailing my arms against these monsters. I didn't have a weapon. Not even a pen.

There were no policemen on the ground. Nice that the helicopters had arrived. Where were the policemen? Shoes on the ground?

What did a twisted sadist like Hannibal have in mind? He'd ordered a knife up Homburg hat's anus. And a knife up between Irina's legs. The knife up an anus signaling disgust that Homburg hat had chased boys instead of contacting Coyotes! A knife up between Irina's legs!

Oh, Hannibal knew that this dangerous witness had worked in a brothel. But Happy? In this crowd?

My friendly taxi driver finished his *taquiero*. Offering him that treat in a tent had possibly saved me from being spotted by Hannibal. We'd dined together in Oxfordshire, he'd recognize me in a T-shirt without being in black tie.

I tried out two words that are the same in English and Spanish: "Radio? Police?"

My driver nodded. He'd caught my drift, left me and was last seen back in his taxi on its radio calling the police.

Onlookers poured in-and-out like a sea that couldn't settle on a shore. The bikers weren't the sole attraction. In line with its publicity as a Festival, miniature fair ground treats had magnetized a growing number of the public. There were shooting booths: "Win a plush dog." No shooting Happy there. Wouldn't be imaginative enough for Hannibal.

I saw a cotton candy stand. Colored balloons.

There was a fly-about that whirled child-sized space ships fifty feet off the ground.

More importantly, a wedding party arrived in full splendor. In addition to a bride in an Elizabethan-style gown wearing a tiara to hold her billowing veil, and an amorous groom in black tie sporting an Edwardian velvet jacket, there were numerous relations and well-dressed guests. A red carpet marked the way for these relations and guests to attend various entertainments prior to the actual religious ceremony.

Included was a bower of out-of-season flowers, mostly Victorian roses. Beyond it was a maze, created by box wood planted in versailles containers.

There was a carousel. It was a veritable antique, with hand-painted horses that rose and fell thanks to a contraption through the middle of each horse. The wedding party's children, the flower girl and ring boy, expensively kitted out as Seventeenth Century courtiers for the occasion, quickly took over the carousel, holding staunchly to the horses' reins, and giggling self-consciously as they waved to the bride and groom. A long line of patiently-waiting wedding guests stood in front of the carousel waiting their turn.

That must be it!

Hannibal planned to kill my wife on that merry-go-round; Happy, a jockey, would be knifed on a carousel horse. Hannibal would consider *that* appropriate.

I saw that Happy noticed the carousel, but knowing her every mannerism, I recognized Happy's strategy as she leaned away from the carousel and towards the bikers. On many a racetrack Happy had eluded jockeys' mounts by that strategy. It was the old double-take: pretending to get away from a pack of horses to have a free run to the Finish, while actually leaning in toward the marauding horses, only to sprint back toward the opening she'd gained. She'd won her race in Japan with that maneuver.

But, here? With her body against the side of a master killer? That old double-take must prove to no avail.

I'd forgotten that Happy used a different facet as a jockey in a long race rather than a sprint.

She tore from between the two killers. Boris flashed his knife. Too late! Happy had swerved TOWARD the carousel, backtracked to a group of bikers, snatched a bike and was pedaling as if nearing the Finish of the Tour de France. She inched into the safe center of a mass of bikers heading for the Golden Gate park's exit.

Two trails on offer detailed their routes by newly designed signs. Happy chose the shortest route. It was a loop trail, with shade trees bordering the road.

I grabbed my driver, we sped to his taxi and hit that road. He drove carefully to keep up with Happy without passing her.

Up, up the bikers went. They were familiar with this challenging route. But could Happy hope to keep up with them?

There were other non-bikers on the road. A van, with CBS TV written on its side, pulled along the route at the same speed as the bikers were managing. A red roadster, more befitting a lazy ocean-side spin, sported crates of bottles of water. Without stopping, or slowing, these bikers grabbed a bottle from the roadster's passengers' ready hands and sped on.

Happy, on a turn, saw me in the taxi. Sliding out of the bike's saddle as if she'd just won a maiden race, she chortled: "Hi, Rick-Honey. Ain't had so much fun since ourn honeymoon."

She climbed into the taxi, we crushed into each other, and I whispered: "Thank you, God."

Chapter 19

With Hannibal and Boris arrested, I felt we must rush back to the two little illegals.

Again no trouble at the border crossing. As our taxi driver was well-known and liked by these evening hour guards, Happy, in her soiled Mexico City trousers, drew nothing more than: "Enjoy your stay in Mexico, little lady."

We'd regained Mexico!

I knew that she must be extremely tired, hungry, and thirsty. We stopped at a taqueria that our driver chose. He hadn't forgotten my offer at a taqueria in Golden Hill Park. He'd paid me back a thousand times over for that taco, but he still wanted to treat us to an authentic made-in-Mexico taco.

Happy needed to go pee more than she wanted a taco. That accomplished, she sat down opposite me and told me why she'd gone to trap Hannibal.

"It were lahke this," she began. "From Ox-fordshire, Ah'd known he be a billionaire. Told in Ox-fordshire he were on the Forbes 500 List. He done told me he needed help t'stop Coyotes from connin' Cen-tral 'Merican kids outta $7000 dollahs. Promisin' t' git 'em ac-ross the U-nited States border. Why me?"

"Maybe because you're so pretty!" I said that as a joke, but I meant it.

"Yo-all re-call how he done come late to thet fancy dinner? Dressed in shootin' clothes propah fo' shootin' pheasants? He wanted to show-off to all them Embassy swell-heads that he were goin' on the Duke's shoot next mornin'. Yup, while they-uns had to sit through some lec-ture about them Coyotes. He is one big SHOW-Off. He pre-tended to show how great he were goin' to be to them il-legals. He hired ME 'cause he thought Ah'm a stu-pid woman. He were showin'-off, sayin' he'd pay fo' a sleuth to git on the trails o' Coyotes."

"Go on."

"We gits money, tickets, but no ad-vice. Already leavin' the airpoht we gits mugged. Cheap try t' warn us off? Could 'ave killed us. Why-all didn't he order thet done theah, in Mexico City! 'Cause he be such a Show-off, he want to show he weren't cheap, he'd hired a comp'tent puhson. Then thet Maserati cah with them baddies done shown up. Ah's thinkin': mebbe there be mo'e t'this than trappin' a few Coyotes."

"More? Like what!"

"No idee. Not then, not until Ciudad Juarez. Got me mo'e o' an inklin' in Columbus. Yo-all recall Hannibal 'phoned me theah?"

"I'm not likely to forget. We'd just made love, and were about to enjoy rapture with a second afterglow."

"Yeah-man. Well, thet Hannibal, he made a mis-take. He fo'got thet iPhones show the name and place o' who be callin'. Mine said Hannibal Kalashnikov, Columbus, New Mexico, U.S.A, and gave his private iPhone numbuh. Yeah man, he be in the *SAME* TOWN AS WE BE, 'N PRETENDIN' HE BE IN WASHINGTON! Then he done showed a diff-er-ent side. His money side. The Show-off's money side. He'd had Homburg hat trackin' us, 'n he got the idee Ah wuz in Mexico fo' money, not fo' savin' il-legal kids. So he sees me as a po-tential pardner. Me! With three kids o' mah own. Kids Ah adores, waitin' fo' me at home. The show-off, he tells me how he made his billions. Yup, billions. In oil, in Russia, 'cause he be born in Russia 'n built up his bus'ness theah. Moved t'Ox-fordshire so's he could git t'keep his money."

"That worked. He seems to have kept it."

"Yeah, but lahke so many o' them billionaires, al-ways wants more. 'N he needed t'keep Pres-i-dent Putin on his side. So he cooks up a scheme t'git hunderds o' thousands o' extra il-legals swarmin' into the U-nited States. Idee bein' t'give the U-ni-ted States govern-ment somethin' else t' think about than Ukraine."

"God! You may be on to something."

"Sho. Yo-all recalls how Pres-i-dent Putin put on a $50 million Olym-pics in Sochi. We's watchin' them ath-letes on TV while HE grabs the Crimea. With all its oil rights over one-third o' the Black

Sea. Yeah! Same so't o' trick with this-heah im-migration problem. Pres-i-dent Obama already talkin' 'bout spendin' $40 billion fo' mo'e im-migration judges, border patrol agents, 'n how t'feed 'n house them il-legals."

"And you almost got yourself killed."

"Theah be mo'e to Mr. Show-off. He be lahke his friend Pres-i-dent Putin 'cause he says one thing when he's doin' somethin' else."

"I'd hate to have him as an owner of a racehorse."

"He weren't nevuh plannin' t'git rid o' them Coyotes. He pays them to git il-legals across so's they keep comin' with their kids, 'n worse, *collects Coyotes 'n pays them to smuggle ISIS TERRORISTS* across the border."

"TERRORISTS?"

"WHO KNOWS BETTER HOW TO SMUGGLE MEN, WOMEN, 'n CHILLUN THAN COYOTES? 'N mo'e il-legals them Coyotes git across ourn borduhs, easier it be to smuggle Terrorists into the U.S.A."

"God almighty!"

"Hannibal be payin' the noospapuhs in Guat'mala, El Salv'dor 'n Hond'ros to publish sto-ries tellin' folks what a great idee it is to send ambi-tious relatives to the U-nit-ed States. He don't want them Coyotes to go into 'nother business. Hannibal know that mo-e business fo' them Coyotes, mo'e chance to mix TERRORISTS in with a big crowd."

"I'm getting the picture. But, why did President Putin use Hannibal? Such a neurotic show-off?"

"Money. Ain't most rotten deals 'bout money? Putin helped Kash make his in oil, and then came pay-back tahme. Pres'-i-dent Putin, he won't give up tryin' t'git Ukraine back into Russia. He plan way ahead. Yo-all c'n be sho thet when he per-mitted Hannibal to make 'n keep his oil money, he'd already figured out Russia should send 'sleepers' across the southern bohduh of the U-ni-ted States. He tell Hannibal to sho'ten his Kalashnikov name to Kash, 'n gave him the job to r'cruit as many Coyotes as possible."

"And you, my darling, were plumbing for this information those long ten hours in Columbus?"

"Sho thing. Took some doin' but Ah kept tellin' mahself it were no mo'e dang'rous than ridin' in a twenty-hoss race."

"Yes, my darling. You would!"

"Ah spent all thet time in the ho-tel's computer room. Had me a sandwich half way through. I were into nine 'n three quartuh hours sittin' theah when Ah nailed him. Yeah man! Ah'd been countin' on his being such a Show Off. Ah's plumbed Google, Twitter, 'n Blog, but it were on his Facebook page wheah he made a mis-take. He boasted his success had always depended on his clever picking of the right people he needed for his pro-jects. Why had he picked me? 'Cause Ah'd caught ser-ial killers. So, he needed serial killers. What fo'? To use them as Coyotes to smuggle terr-o-rists into the U.S.A. Killers who shoot first 'n no questions asked."

"My darling Happy! You knew this and yet continued to track him!"

"Ah's a U.S. cit'zen 'n this show-Off were en-dangerin' mah country. But Ah does turribly re-gret Ah weren't able to trap him be-fo'e he killed Irina."

"Irina was ex-KGB. She'd probably guessed what was up. She knew she'd be dead when she made a threesome with us. I'm deeply sorry about Irina. But, my darling, I'm really grateful it wasn't *you* with that knife between her beautiful legs." I was feeling as gauche as a bridegroom arriving late to his own wedding.

"Thet were't nevuh goin' t'happen. Mah special place be mah heart, 'n Rick-Honey it be yourn. 'Nuf o' Hannibal talk. Let's usn eat."

Happy tore into the taco on her plate as if she was a Mexican kid on vacation.

When she'd finished, my driver paid for our tacos, and drove us to our hotel. I paid him double what WE'D AGREED, gave him the largest tip I've ever parted with, and also invited him to eat dinner with us at our hotel.

He understood enough English to appreciate the invitation. Shook his head. "No, señor. *Tengo mi esposa esperandome en la cama.*" And *I* understood that!

I wanted *my* wife in bed with *me*. "Let's leave Angela and Flor in the convent school for tonight," I whispered into Happy's delicious ear. I loved to lick that ear, and after we both had showers together, I did.

When we were drifting on a sex-produced raft through a most delicious afterglow, I thought: isn't it true you appreciate more what you thought you'd lost?

Chapter 20

The nuns at the convent school were still at Matins when we went to collect Angela and Flor. Sister Benedicta informed us after Matins that there would be a delay of some minutes before we could see them.

HAPPY USED THE OPPORTUNITY TO ASK ANOTHER NUN TO TELEPHONE THE GIRLS' GRANDMOTHER. With her help Happy managed to speak to the grandmother, who'd been the initiator of the plan to send Angela and Flor across Mexico to the United States border. She spoke some English.

The helpful nun passed her telephone's receiver to Happy. In broken English the grandmother's voice ripped down the line. "You want me come to Guatemala City? Today? Aurora Airport! But I have doctor appointment. No matter, I break. I be there, meet your airplane from Mexico City." She never mentioned a mother of either of the girls.

But she sounded relieved that the girls were coming back home. No doubt she'd had a negative reply from her son to her pleas -- the girls' unwilling uncle – and now knew there would be no welcome for Angela and Flor in Chicago.

Sister Benedicta skipped breakfast to deliver the girls to us. She didn't hug them.

She must have told Angela to strip their beds, because Angela was busy doing exactly that. As we watched, Angela folded the sheets and pillowcases and placed them into a bin for dirty laundry. Mother Antonia had probably warned Sister Benedicta about Angela's lice and Flor's too-recent scabies.

With great care not to crease the tissue paper, the good nun returned their organdy dresses to each girl, still in the dry cleaning bags.

We thanked Sister Benedicta, gave an offering for a memorial mass for Irina, and sped in a new taxi to Tijuana's airport.

Angela, ecstatic to be on her way home and to be reunited there with her grandmother, sang a little song when she realized she was going to be flying in an airplane. Flor, wanting her mother more than her grandmother, acted terrified to board an airplane. She started her weeping again.

Happy worked her motherly skills, bought another Mexican china poblana doll for Flor, not forgetting to spend an equal amount on a gift for their grandmother to be presented by Angela.

Our flight was uneventful, except that both children asked and got a second luncheon tray. Their stay in the convent school may have been sanitary and safe, but they can't have been fed very generously.

Perhaps that wasn't a very kind thought on my part: it had been our urgency to get to the airport that had made the girls miss breakfast.

While we'd waited for the girls' trip to Guatemala to be called, we'd renewed our flight tickets to leave for England that same night. We were going to accompany the girls on their final journey, therefore the planes to and from Guatemala had to be strictly on time. There was a very narrow window between our arriving back from Guatemala and taking off for England.

Hour after hour on route to Guatemala we flew over green fields and well manicured ranches. Happy remarked: "Don't look like there be no gang vi-o-lence in these pahts."

I agreed. "It wasn't really necessary for the girls to leave their homes. Think what a terribly long journey the girls had to take by various buses to go seventeen hundred miles to reach Juarez City."

We landed on time and hurried to be first off the plane. "Abuelita," Angela sang out from the Arrivals gate. Like a bullet she sped to reach a frail, stooped, elderly peasant woman.

Flor held back. She didn't want her pristine dry cleaning bag to be crushed with its precious cargo of her organdy dress. Eventually, an overwhelming desire to show off the dress and her Mexican doll propelled Flor to share the woman's arms with Angela.

The woman singled out my wife. In fractured English she breathed hard out of sick lungs: "Many thanks I give to you."

That was it. The two girls waved at us, remembered to send a mouthed "Thank you," and then the three headed to the lounge for passengers on the next flight to the Petin Airport near the far hills where they lived.

My darling Happy proceeded to indulge her passion for shopping. Aurora Airport had plenty of stores. Happy found an elegant Guatemalan chalina for Elga. She got a stuffed monkey for Richard, a book full of pictures of Mexico's wildlife for Tim, and another china poblana doll for Dorothy, this one incorrectly wearing an oversized sombrero atop her braids. As usual, I bought nothing.

Elga came to Mexico City's airport to hear our news and wish us God Speed, hoping that we'd have enough time between flights to visit together. No orangutan. Maybe she felt that night air didn't work with Martica's standard routine. Our generous Mexico City hostess had aged in the few days since our departure. She was stooped like a Halloween witch.

"I've worried so much for the two of you. I read Happy's e-mail. It was impossible for me to learn what happened *after* she sent it. I can't begin to tell you how relieved I felt when Happy's phone call alerted you'd be changing planes here. How did she get away from those men? And WHY a plane to and from Guatemala?"

The tannoy loudspeaker was calling our London flight. "Call you from England," Happy breathed through a kiss, and handed the unwrapped chalina to Elga. I waved from the departure gate, it closed, we sped through a down-leaning tunnel, boarded, and swiftly located the First Class seats Hannibal -- that show-off -- had provided.

Before we took off, I scanned The Daily Mail to check whether Happy's saga had made the front page. It hadn't.

Chapter 21

Arriving home at Epson, we both felt relieved to learn that both Hannibal Kash and Boris had been arrested in the U.S.A. Happy ran forward to hug all three children.

"Chillun, lookee heah wut Mom's brought yo-all!" Happy well knew that gifts were expected by our kids after a week's absence. They didn't ask ME for anything. They knew I hated shopping.

We'd hardly come to the end of our driveway when all three of our kids came trumpeting out of our thatched roof cottage. Nanny was not far behind them, hovering like a guardian angel.

Tim was quick to scan the book on Mexico's wildlife. "Who cares about monkeys and macaws? Why couldn't I have a book on the interstellar Aliens that landed there? Lots of sightings of Aliens in Mexico."

No whining from Richard. He embraced his stuffed monkey, while simultaneously yanking at its tail. The tail came off. So much for Mexican handicrafts! Dorothy's doll had a similar fate. The sombrero fell off, revealing a bare pate of hideous pink plastic. The braids grew out of it like small dragons. Never mind, Dorothy firmly planted the doll under one armpit and rushed to give Happy a smoochy kiss.

Thank goodness the nanny's gift was in our collection of gifts, not swallowed up in Happy's suitcase. Happy presented it to her with a flourish, like when our noble Monarch hands out the prizes at Royal Ascot.

A coffee addict, who stayed up half the night watching our kids due to all that caffeine, Nanny was delighted with her present. It was a Mexican coffee pot that came with a pound of Mexico's finest makeable brew.

I took Tim with me to check on morning stables. Joe, our great Head Lad, lurked inside ARROW's stall, Gruffly, he got right to business: Tom was very used to our sudden trips. We'd taken him with us when we raced a difficult horse that performed only for Tom. 'Mr. Harrow, we'd best call the Vet. This poor fellow got a sore foreleg."

Keeping Tim well away from the stall, I slipped inside to test the foreleg. "Vet it is. You call him, Tom. And thank you for watching over our string these last fraught days."

"Yes *Sir*. I seen Mrs Harrow's e-mail. Most folks 'round the world seen it. My guess is that Lord Cabrach must wish as he'd never introduced you both to that Hannibal person."

Jeremy stood in the stable's doorway. "Heard your car come down the drive. Welcome back, Rick. Tom's got that absolutely right. I DO truly eat humble pie. You, Tom, will have to give me tips in future on the horses I should bet on. I certainly read Hannibal wrong."

We slapped each other's shoulders and after a quick look-see of the other horses in my string, I led Jeremy to our cottage.

Happy was already standing in the doorway, a kitchen apron over her soiled linen trousers. 'Hi yo-all. Jeremy, WANT SOME LUNCH?"

"Yes, please. And the whole Hannibal story."

I handed Jeremy a glass of Pinot Noir.

"Huh. Well, to staht, he not be English. Shootin' pheasants with the duke were a con. He be a Russian billionaire, palsy with Pres-i-dent Putin. Togethuh they cooked up a plan t' make the U-nited States spend billions in-stead of millions on the illegal im-mi-grants swarmin' t'America. Billions spent to safeguard ourn Southern border, 'n feed them kids without folks wut come. Soft-hearted 'Merican votuhs wuz cryin' about these po'r li'l illegal kids. But there be mo'e. He needed killuhs t'act as Coyotes to get Terr-or-rists across the borduh mixed in with all them Latino illegals."

Jeremy, with his background in the M-I5, said: "Happy, Hannibal lied when he asked you to help him get rid of Coyotes?"

"Sho did. In-stead of gettin' rid o' Coyotes, Hannibal were payin' them mo'e than the drug dealuhs had. He re-cruited killuhs t'use Coyote tricks. Hannibal spent millions to make 'Merica spend billions. He paid off po-lice. Paid noospapuhs in Guat'mala, Hond'ras 'n El Sal-va-dor fo' edi-torials t' encourage folk t'let them kids leave home alone. Paid to hi-jack drones fo' Coyotes t'know the sa-fest routes. Paid fo' tunnels unduh barriers. Paid fo' boats t'cross the Rio Grande."

"Will Hannibal be able to pay his way out of being the intellectual author of two murders?"

"Sho 'nuf. He gonna pay fo' th'best lawyers, but he weren't so smart t'get Irina's mobile with Homburg hat's picture, finguhprints 'n DNA. Same with his Mas'rati. Finguh prints 'n DNA o' his, Boris's 'n Hombug hat's. All tie him t'the two murduhs. But Ah's bettin' if he go to pri-son, his pal Pres'dent Putin gits him ex-changed fo' some 'Merican thet the Russians be holdin'. Yeah man. Even when the government re-alizes thet Hannibal were payin' Coyotes to sneak TERRORISTS across ourn borduhs!"

"Happy, that's one bet nobody will take."

"Wanna heah mo'e?" Happy felt ready to talk out all that had been going through her mind.

But Tim, Dorothy and Richard wanted to eat dinner. They went into our dining niche and sat down, signaling they wanted food.

Happy left Jeremy and me to our drinks, decided not to enlarge on the events of the past week, went to the kitchen, and helped Nanny by carrying the ketchup for a steaming cottage pie to the children.

With Happy, kids always came first.

end